Joanna ran a

spoke again she wa

her arms. "I don't want this on," she said. "There isn't anyone for miles. And, anyway, it's petty. A littleness of people against the rest of it here. Without our clothes we're a part of the universe."

"It's a good line, Joey."

"It feels marvelous." She was lying back on the hot sand, luxurious, her arms under her head.

Naked, it did feel marvelous. Indulged. Uncluttered.

After a while I slightly parted her legs so that I could lie between them, propped on my elbows, looking at her, knowing that soon we would make love, in some odd way enjoying the postponement. . . .

I suppose I have never believed that one human being can possess another, not really. We belong only to ourselves. But that late morning in the sun I had the feeling that, incredibly, wonderfully, she was mine — that "Let me . . ." was no part of it, that anything from love I would want to do would be allowed, welcomed, responded to.

"Do you know — did I ever tell you? — that just sometimes I can feel the throbbing inside you."

She laughed softly, drawing me down with her arms so that we were close against each other, moving, she was kissing my mouth, saying against it, "I love you" . . . and we made love, with passion, and a new abandon.

When it was over, the taste of her on my tongue, my whole consciousness suffused with the faint, marvelous smell of her skin, the feel and touch of her, we lay silent on the sand.

The Bee's Kiss

by Shirley Verel

The Bee's Kiss

by Shirley Verel

The Naiad Press, Inc.
1989

Copyright © 1989 by Shirley Verel

All rights reserved. No part of this book may be reproduced or transmitted in any form or by any means electronic or mechanical without permission in writing from the publisher.

Printed in the United States of America
First Edition

Edited by Christi Cassidy
Cover design by Pat Tong and Bonnie Liss
(Phoenix Graphics)
Typeset by Sandi Stancil

Library of Congress Cataloging-in-Publication Data

Verel, Shirley.
The bee's kiss.

I. Title.
PR6072.E58B4 1989 823.914 88-29150
ISBN 0-941483-36-3 (pbk.)

The Bee's kiss, now!
Kiss me as if you entered gay
My heat at some noonday . . .

Robert Browning

To J-C

About the Author

Shirley Verel, author of *The Other Side of Venus,* reprinted by Naiad Press in 1988, lives in London. *The Bee's Kiss* is her first novel since she completed *The Other Side of Venus* in 1960. She is presently engaged in writing another lesbian novel for The Naiad Press.

ONE

It isn't always that people live up to expectations but in the case of Joanna I think it would be fair to say she had a tendency to exceed them. Certainly the first day I actually took in the fact of her existence did nothing to alter this idea.

What else I could say of her with equal conviction I'm not sure. There have been times when I have wondered whether I ever really knew her, ever really understood her. What I'm quite sure of is that while in some ways she was the most intense sexual experience of all my life, a lifetime where in the event love had turned out to be the one thing to rival the coercions of writing, never for a moment did I feel that I possessed her.

It is a loose expression, of course — what do I mean by possess? To be not only safely at the center of someone else's passion, but to have in it a controlling interest? I don't know. But, anyway, I do know I have wondered about the other relationships she will have had in her life, wondering about them the way we often do go on wondering about stories that have never quite been finished for us.

The beginning of this story, I remember: it was cold, the surprising cold of an early winter. In some pocket of memory I remember being surprised the hedges should already have had something of a threadbare look.

Walking home from the library I wished I had brought the car, but not without knowing perfectly well why I hadn't. "Managing" had taken economies and one of them was usually leaving the car in the garage.

I was twenty-four, I had been a widow for a year and two months, and my son had just started school.

What strikes me, looking back after so long at my situation then, is the sheer statistical improbability of it, besides how young it was for me to marry and have a baby.

At the time, following the first shock, the mechanisms of reaction and feeling had in some curious way seemed simply to seize up.

The walk took about twenty minutes. Home was the upstairs of a large house on the outskirts of Whitethorn, a country town just about within commuting distance of London. A few months before Tom had been killed climbing Sco Peak, we had bought the house for informal sharing with Cassie and Peter Turner, friends of ours. Or, to be more precise, friends of his. The sharing had continued though perhaps rather more separately than before.

Our hall had a faint, agreeable smell of Cassie's cooking. I went into their sitting room and found Peter on the phone. "Well, doesn't anybody know where she is now?" he was saying.

He looked up briefly at me. "Joanna," he explained, but I couldn't think who Joanna was.

Not wanting to appear to involve myself in his conversation I stood for a moment by the fire, which was spilling out hotly, gray and red, from the grate, and glanced round the room. A reading lamp, already switched on, and made out of the wooden model of a yacht, threw its small, neat egg of light onto the bare wall over the bookshelves.

"Oh, God," Peter said.

Clearly his conversation was nowhere near its end and equally clearly, I thought, hadn't anything to do with me. I picked up a sodden painting book and a paste pot of blackish water from the floor, then went over to him.

"Where's Hugh?" I asked, murmuring it.

"Alison's," he said, and returned to his phoning.

* * * * *

Alison was my friend at Whitethorn as well as especially Cassie's. She lived in a converted water tower at the unbelievable top of which she had a studio where she illustrated up-market children's books with conspicuous success. The tower had softish yellow brick and a long history which was quite interesting if you happened to be in the mood. I had once heard her say of her husband, "Don't ask James about The Tower. He'll tell you." She had a way of giving to what she said an ironic, slightly caustic edge which at that stage of my life I had found strangely acceptable, even somehow comforting. I couldn't have explained why.

The light was on in the huge windowed studio, the front door wasn't locked, and I climbed the endless, turning stairs.

Alison appeared to be tidying rather than working. She just missed looking severe and looked elegant instead. Her clothes were elegant, her prematurely silver hair was done in what used to be called a "French twist" — I have no idea what it is called now — and her spectacles were bold and unrepentant. When she saw me she put down the handful of drawings she was holding.

"I thought Hugh was with you."

"He was. James has taken him out to tea. James is of the opinion that mid-term holidays should be marked in some such fashion."

"*I* was going to do something. Only I had to go to the library first, there was something I had to look up, and he didn't want to come to the library."

"Don't be defensive, Roz. And sit down a minute. After you've helped yourself to a drink, of course. You must know the stairs are an automatic entitlement. Didn't Peter tell you about James?"

"He didn't tell me about anything. He was tied up with some telephone drama. Joanna. Who's that, do you know?"

"Cassie's niece." Alison sat down. "In a manner of speaking. I believe it's a step-brother. Why?"

Even then I wasn't sure I could have placed the name. I knew Cassie had a step-brother whose name was Arnold. "I don't know why. I don't know anything about it. It seemed to be something to do with not knowing where she was."

At this, Alison said that Joanna was at boarding school, the mother having wandered off with someone else, hadn't Cassie said? And when I shook my head she commented, "You don't seem to know much about your housemate's relatives."

"No, but why would I?"

"All good copy."

It was one of Alison's little jokes that if you had written even one book, no one anywhere was safe from your remorseless pursuit of "copy." I said, "There's always that, of course. But would I get much from a girls' boarding school? Besides, I've never even met Cassie's niece and I don't suppose I ever will. Cassie doesn't get on with her step-brother."

"Anyone who doesn't get on with Cassie must be entirely at fault." Alison finished her drink in a single swallow. "Well, if there's anything exciting to tell, no doubt Cassie will tell it."

She did. She came up to my room after I had put Hugh to bed and what she had to tell somewhat increased my interest in the whole affair if only because it was such a good example of how fatally easy it is to get caught out. Joanna had conveyed the impression to her father, it seemed, that she was going on the mid-term's week-long geography class field trip while informing the school that she wasn't. And the beautiful simplicity of this might even have worked if the geography teacher hadn't at the last moment decided to send some duplicated notes home to those of her senior students who wouldn't be going away with her.

Cassie was a teacher. She taught art at Whitethorn's grammar school. She was the kind of woman whose age was never going to be really important — big, with a mouth which had I been a painter I think I would have wanted to paint. It was an ungrudging mouth, and had already settled into lines of natural kindness. "Of course, Arnold phoned the school," she said. "And now nobody knows who she's with. Or where she is."

"But at any rate it's where she wants to be, apparently. I mean she doesn't seem to have been kidnapped or anything. And she won't even know what's going on here." All at once something in me, however inappropriately, wanted to laugh. "She's probably intending just to come back at the end of the week as if nothing had happened."

"She won't be able to do that. It's all extremely worrying. Arnold isn't pleased, to say the least. And he always has so many business things to see to." Cassie frowned. "Anyway she should have gone on the field trip. She has her A level examinations next summer." There was a pause.

"Cassie, how old is she? Eighteen?" Suddenly I was interested.

"At the end of the year."

"Still, by now I suppose the charms of boarding school could be wearing a bit thin — she's certainly not a child any more."

"That opens up such an array of possibilities," Cassie said, "I don't like to think about it."

"Oh, come on, it isn't as if she's been discovered in a ditch. Anyway, what's Arnold going to do?"

"He hasn't decided. It felt to me as if he'd like to wash his hands of her. He certainly doesn't want a lot of publicity."

* * * * *

But whatever Arnold wanted or didn't want, by the next day the papers had got hold of it.

TWO

One of them was purposefully brought in to me by the "help" — it was what she called herself — Cassie and I shared along with the house. Parting with Mrs. Carnaby should have been one of the economies, but it was awkward and I had gone on putting it off.

Now, short, energetic, responding to the moment, she stood there, holding the paper open and saying, "Look at that. Just look at that! Some brute taking advantage of an innocent girl, you can bet your life."

I had been trying to do some writing while Hugh was playing with a line of little boats I had bought him and would rather not have been interrupted but neither she nor the news gave me any option. The headline read: FEARS FOR CONVENT GIRL. Under it was a photograph. "I only hope the girl comes out of this alive," Mrs. Carnaby was saying. "Poor Mrs. T's terribly bothered."

"Mrs. Carnaby," Hugh was calling from the bathroom. "Mrs. Carnaby, come and see my boats."

She looked at me as much as to say, What can I do? When she was gone I studied the photograph. It appeared to have been blown up from a group shot and was quite unfinished but the girl, I thought, seemed rather beautiful. She had darkish hair a little less than shoulder length, and nice teeth. Her look was direct yet somehow, in some odd fashion, as if not giving much away.

Mrs. Carnaby returned to enlarge on possible disasters.

When the vacuuming began I folded the newspaper and put it among some things of mine, hoping that she wouldn't reclaim it. But I had no idea why.

Peter had his own copy of a different newspaper. It had preferred MISSING for FEARS FOR and there was no photograph but all the same it had concocted three or four paragraphs out of no more than a couple of facts.

"How did they find out anything?"

"Instinct. A whiff of sex and they swoop. This must have been a easy one for them, anyway. Someone at the school knee-jerked a call to the police to ask advice. And once the story has got outside the —"

"That was a bit silly, wasn't it? So soon. It's really only to do with Arnold." Or Joanna, I caught myself thinking.

"Maybe the school hasn't had much practice in such matters. Anyhow, Arnold's at the boiling point now. To be fair, he has had woman trouble before."

"Do you detect a whiff of sex?"

"I'm an open-minded man, Roz, but I can't say alternative explanations have been crowding in."

"What is she like?" (*I asked Peter what Joanna was like.*)

"Her mother."

"That doesn't mean a lot to me."

"Tall. Attractive, of course, but I wouldn't have said she was all that forthcoming with it. Not that I really know anything at all about her. Cassie never saw much of them. For a start Arnold was so much older. And he and Cassie are hardly peas out of a pod."

Seated on the edge of my kitchen table, he went on talking about them, I began to have the feeling that unlike Mrs. Carnaby his sole purpose was not just to discuss the newspaper report, but that he was leading up to something else, was going to ask something. I had that feeling.

He remarked that Joanna and her parents had lived in Bristol before her mother had left and gone to live in Bermuda, and that then Arnold had moved to London and Joanna had gone to boarding school. "After that Arnold seemed positively to discourage any contact. Cassie felt it was because he thought she'd be a bad influence. Too many liberal ideas. It's different at the moment, though, of course. Cassie's really the only woman around."

It was then that he neared his point. "She feels someone ought to go to the school. Talk the matter over. She thinks Joanna ought to do her Advanced Level examinations, whatever else. And Arnold's not exactly in a helpful and constructive mood. Only she's a bit deterred by the thought of tackling a Reverend Mother. She says she isn't into convents."

I waited.

He ran a hand through his reddish hair. "She wanted me to go with her," he said. "But I can't, can I? Well, I *could.* I took this week off to fit in with Cassie's mid-term break. That's a laugh, the way it's turned out. But it wouldn't be very suitable. Me there talking about Joanna. I mean, I've absolutely nothing to do with her."

"I suppose not."

"As a matter of fact, I was wondering if you'd go with Cassie. Back her up." He looked at me.

"Me?" Whatever I might have thought he was going to ask, it wasn't this. "Peter, I've even more absolutely nothing to do with her! I —"

"No, I know. But two women. It would be better, wouldn't it?"

"I couldn't even think who it was when you said Joanna. And I'm not into convents, either. I don't think I've ever spoken to a nun."

At this he laughed. "You know what Alison would say, don't you? You must never turn down useful copy. Go on, Roz. It isn't particularly far. You could get there in an hour. And I'd take Hugh fishing."

So in the end the net result of all that was that Cassie and I drove out through the nice, unself-conscious little village of Meering where Mrs. Carnaby lived, and after about an hour, as Peter had said, arrived at Joanna's convent.

* * * * *

On the main gates was a brass plate lettered with the words CONVENT OF MARY AND JOSEPH. Beyond the gates I could see two buildings, one modern and bare-looking, the other with its ancient grayness heightened in the October sunshine. We approached the older building and Cassie knocked on the door. A few moments passed before we found ourselves facing the first nun I had ever really encountered.

She was small and round-faced, and she wore a long black habit with a stiffened, tight-fitting wimple. The habit looked dusty, and I should think it almost certainly was, it was so long, but her ruff collar, made in some light-weight, pleated material, was very white. She had something circling her waist which rattled warningly when she moved. I supposed it was a rosary, and the thought struck me that if all the nuns wore one of these there must have been times when the younger pupils found it invaluable as a warning.

Her expression changed perceptibly when she learned who we were. It had been friendly, benign almost. She said that she would go and tell the Reverend Mother we were here, and invited us into the hall.

No doubt convent boarding schools, along with most boarding schools, along with attitudes generally, and the rest of life, have become transformed over the past decades.

Perhaps the reason why I recall this one with such clarity — verging on the painful — is that in essence it was where my relationship with Joanna began.

Left alone there, Cassie and I stood looking about us. I was immediately aware of a room, its door open, which had been turned into a chapel. There were flowers on the altar, and two nuns knelt in the plain wooden pews. In the hall itself there were several religious statues, among them a stark crucifix, and one of the Virgin in sky blue.

On a small table by the door, and looking oddly out of place, stood a telephone.

As we waited for the return of the round-faced nun, we were passed from time to time by other members of the order. Several came down from upstairs together, young ones, talking with hushed, girlish animation, and I vaguely remembered having heard somewhere that the only men allowed upstairs in a convent were doctors and plumbers. Then, as my thoughts turned to Joanna, another nun emerged from the room next to the chapel, hand-in-hand with a child.

This nun was very old, eighty or more I should think, though so much of her was covered up that it wasn't easy to tell. The child was certainly not yet eight.

The thing I noticed first about that child was that she was wearing black stockings, and that her skirt was below the knees. In her free hand she was clasping a small, colored picture, very red and gold. She held it up to admire it, and as she went out of the front door with the old nun made some pleased observation.

Shortly afterwards, our nun returned. "Mother will see you now," she said, and having led us along a corridor which branched off from the hall, she showed us into a room overlooking the gardens at the back of the house.

It was a large room, rather plain and cheerless it seemed to me, with two or three upright mahogany chairs and one quite horrible stove. "Please sit down," she told us, and withdrew.

We waited perhaps ten minutes for the appearance of the Reverend Mother, and as we waited I stared idly out of the window, for there was nothing else to do. A severe-looking woman, perhaps in her forties, passed by reading a book.

Nothing further occurred to attract my attention. The garden remained deserted, and I began to feel on edge, curiously oppressed. There felt to me after a time something almost vacuum-like about the room.

"There's nothing to look at."

"Well, it isn't a dentist's waiting room," Cassie said.

"I wasn't expecting *Vogue*. But there isn't even a pattern on the rug."

Finally the Reverend Mother came. To look at she was, I suppose, exactly as one might have imagined a Reverend Mother to be — tall, assured, alabaster-complexioned. I somehow didn't take to her, and wondered at the affectionate, almost fawning manner of her small, round-faced subordinate. She dismissed the nun as if addressing a child, and advanced towards us with a white, fastidiously kept hand outstretched.

"Mrs. Turner?" she inquired of Cassie, and added, "I believe you are a friend," before saying, "This is a very disgraceful affair."

"Yes," said Cassie, clearly not wanting to get off on the wrong foot. "But we don't know all the circumstances yet, do we, and —"

"I'm afraid we do." The Reverend Mother didn't waste any time. "Joanna Patterson's father has been in communication with me. The girl has been traced."

"Where is she?" — Cassie spoke at once.

The Reverend Mother hesitated, as if deciding how much more to disclose, then disregarding Cassie's question she continued, "While the deception itself was bad enough, the purpose it was meant to serve is something quite beyond what this school could involve itself in."

We looked at her.

Cassie tried again. "What has happened?"

"No doubt your brother, Mrs. Turner, will be in touch with you." Once more she paused. "Both he and I feel that it would not be possible now for her to return to the school. What arrangements he will wish to make for her I must of course leave to him."

"I see." That was all, now, that Cassie said, and I had the feeling I understood why. She didn't want to solicit this Reverend Mother for information, still less to argue with her.

"And so it seems that there is very little for you and I to discuss." The Reverend Mother's manner maintained its distance. "I am very sorry this has happened. Joanna is an intelligent girl, but fifteen was not an ideal age for her to have come to us."

It wasn't long after this that Cassie and I were invited to take our leave. My last memory was of her glancing at a small silver watch suspended somewhere within the folds of her robe.

"Oh God," Cassie said, as we walked towards her car. I remembered it was what Peter had said earlier.

We began to discuss what we had just heard.

Then I said, "Poor Joanna. And what an unbelievable fuss to be making. Suppose she's fallen in love, or she hasn't, it's not cataclysmic. It's not the crack of doom."

"No. Not for us, maybe. But it's hardly the kind of thing a boarding school would take in its stride."

"Cassie, whose side are you on?"

"I'm wondering about who it is she's mixed up with. And what that could mean for anything anybody might try to do to help — retrieve the situation."

"Suppose it's a multi-national bright boy. Wouldn't that please Arnold? Or a bishop's son. Or a wine baron." I said "wine baron" of the top of my head, I don't know why.

"Suppose it's not."

"It could be a poet. Cassie, haven't you ever had an adventure in your life?"

Cassie barely smiled, without replying.

"I'm beginning to feel I'd like to start a hands-off-Joanna-campaign."

As we approached the Whitethorn area we lapsed into silence. The surrounding countryside wasn't at its best in the autumn, and at its showiest it didn't go in much for such things as the groups of thatched cottages that find their way onto picture postcards. It was well off for lanes and orchards, and some of the orchards, with their whitened tree bark, and a smattering of spring and summer flowers, could look seasonally rather pretty. But now it seemed bare and chilly.

It was as we were passing the stone cottage, with its *1905* under the eaves, where Mrs. Hallam, Cassie's headmistress, lived, that Cassie said, "I'm not sure your campaign wouldn't be superfluous. Arnold's going to have had just about enough. I have the feeling he might simply leave her to get on with it, tell her to find a job. He's in a funny frame of mind."

"Or might he try a very heavy father act?"

"That's possible, too."

Cassie turned the car into our driveway. The house we shared had been a vicarage in the days when country vicarages for vicars were more in demand, and it had a long garden that sloped down to the stream which ran through fields at the end of it.

She thanked me for going, which was rather a joke for all the supporting I had done, and which anyhow in some odd way now seemed unnecessary. I would have chosen to go. Then when she was putting her car in the garage I walked down to the stream through the wooden gate which separated it from our garden to see if there was any sign of Hugh returning with Peter.

There wasn't yet. I stood for a moment undecided. The sun had gone, and the willows with the darker trees of the garden had made a half-light. A few insects surviving the autumn that was now so nearly winter skimmed over the water. There was the faint, vague smell of water which in warmer months came together with the smells of the garden to make a wonderful odorousness.

As I stood looking down at the stream I found myself trying to sort out in my mind the day's visit rather than my new novel edging forward (the two processes, perhaps, not so different). This might have told me, I suppose, something had already changed. Joanna, from being not even a name was becoming a reality, a person, someone I thought things about — with however little to go on, apart from imagining.

I wasn't, for instance, particularly surprised that she had been found. Nor, I think, was Cassie, though it was to Arnold Cassie now had to look for further information. I somehow didn't believe that Joanna had been really "running away;" I believed, I think, she had just wanted her own week, conceivably with someone she cared about, conceivably as some sort of early experimentation of the kind I hadn't had. I didn't in my imagining believe that she would have gone unprepared and come back pregnant, or even that she would have been with anyone not also showing a concern for such matters.

But for some reason I was quite sure Arnold was going to be tyrannical and bullying, that he would confuse her disappearance with being left by his wife, and there wasn't much Cassie was going to be able to do. I also thought that for all her belief in passing A Level examinations she now wouldn't want to put her weight behind Joanna's return to the Mary and Joseph Convent.

I tried to think objectively about the convent. What did surprise me, I found, not just in the matter of religion, but when it came to it almost anything else, was that people's convictions could be detailed, so pin-pointed, so seemingly implacable.

And in the end, as I stood there, no attempt to be objective could prevent me from wondering why Arnold had chosen that particular school for his daughter.

I discovered that I was feeling not sorry for her exactly, but had a sense of sympathy for her, fellowship almost — which might have come from the fact that Arnold was a different generation and Cassie, though most of the time I was scarcely aware of it, was nearer his age than mine.

Much later in our story, Joanna remarked to me that she hadn't especially minded her convent, that she and her friends had, as she had put it, made their own amusements, and that as far as the Reverend Mother was concerned they hadn't very often seen her.

"Only brought out for seductions," she had said, looking up at me with the smile to become so familiar, that fell just short of laughter.

I was about to go indoors when I saw James, his evening newspaper under his arm, and called to him on impulse.

"James . . ."

"Yes?" he said, coming towards me.

"James, can you tell me something?"

"That depends, doesn't it? Certainly I am a vast mine of information largely unmarketable." He was a bank manager, but had picked up over the years something of

Alison's way of speaking. "What is it I can do for you? If it's a financial point —"

"No, it isn't. It's legal, really. I wanted to know how long you can be compelled to live at home. How long it is, I mean, before you can live where you like?"

He looked surprised. "Why — are you thinking of leaving?"

I laughed. "No. It's not that. I mean, parents. How long do you have to go on living with your parents, your father? How long can he make you? From a legal point of view."

"Oh, I see." I noticed his glance at the padlock hanging from our garden gate; it was rather as if he had now decided that there could be nothing very important about what I had to ask. "I must say I do feel considerably relieved. I had wondered whatever domestic disaster you could be about to confide. That Hugh had become quite out of hand, perhaps. Well, the answer to your inquiry is perfectly straightforward — sixteen. So long, that is, as there's no question of being exposed to — well, what might be described as improper influences." He rattled the padlock briefly. "That wood's not what it was, either, you know, Roz," he said, fastidious in such matters himself. "I've just been checking mine. Wise to keep an eye. Your wood may not have been too good to start with. I should get Peter to have a look at it."

"Yes, I will. James —"

"One wants to keep one's domestic security arrangements up to the mark," he persisted, and smiled at me.

"Yes. I'll get Peter to look at it. Do you know what the situation would be at seventeen?"

"At seventeen? What situation? There wouldn't be a situation, would there?"

"Well, a girl leaving home and —"

"I can't see the difficulty. Of course, I'm not a lawyer. I suppose there could be complications with matters of abduction and such like." Then suddenly, with a measure of perspicacity, he said, "Oh, are we talking about that niece of Cassie's? As a matter of fact Alison asked me to drop this in to Cassie." He indicated his paper. "There's a bit more in here. I expect she'll have heard."

I glanced at the paper. "What does it say?"

"Oh, I didn't pay a lot of attention. She's been staying in a pub in Suffolk. With a member of Her Majesty's armed forces, it appears, though he seems to have made off somewhere now. Here, Roz, you could take this in to Cassie if you would." He handed me his paper. "She might be mildly interested if she hasn't seen it. It says, I think, one of the regulars recognized her from a photograph."

"Does it say where she is now, James?"

He shrugged. "She reported to a police station."

But even that didn't turn out to be true.

THREE

The idea forming in my mind of Joanna as a person made me think about her and her present situation, but what I had heard hadn't particularly nudged me in the direction of what she herself turned out to have been thinking. To know the real story I had to wait until Arnold came in person to discuss with Cassie his latest news, neither taken from a newspaper nor what any of us had expected.

On the afternoon Arnold came — it was a Thursday, I think — I took Hugh to see one of the Disney films. He had become conscious of his break from school running out, and I had wanted to make an especial fuss of him.

Afterwards, we went to the nearby children's playground. It had a couple of swings and a witch's hat roundabout and not a lot more but, perhaps rather in the way of someone who has had only one lover, Hugh was not critical. Then we started for home.

Hugh had a particular reason for wanting to go home past The Tower.

The Tower's back garden was attached to a field in which was kept a horse. Barbary, a brown and white stallion, had been bought for his daughter by the father of one of Cassie's pupils but had proved to be strikingly unfitted for becoming the soul mate of a tentative twelve-year-old girl, and at the time any attempt to cement the relationship had been in abeyance.

There had been some suggestion that Alison's son, Roger, might be able to exercise a benign influence on the horse, since he had had some experience of riding. He was reading English at London and was expected home for Christmas.

I wouldn't have put money on Roger's influence over Barbary. Barbary was large, with ears that really did flick back, and flanks that really did quiver, and eyes that rolled.

Hugh was fascinated by Barbary. He would stand regarding him for as long as anyone would stand with him, as if mesmerized. It was what he did on this occasion.

"And does he really kick?"

"So the story goes."

"And bite?"

"It is rumored."

"I'd like to ride him."

"In a few years' time."

When we went indoors we could hear Cassie and Arnold talking in the sitting room, and she called me in to meet him. He said "How do you do?" to me, and nodded briefly to Hugh, suggesting that whatever he had it wasn't a way with children.

He looked like a man in a hurry to be off to Zurich who was being delayed by some matter that simply couldn't be shelved, which was in fact the case.

He clearly had no intention of discussing family matters in front of an outsider, and it wasn't until he had gone that I could come downstairs again and ask Cassie what had been happening. She said, "Joanna's phoned him. The police called round to the pub. Just a friendly visit, of course. It couldn't really have been anything else. She was washing up. But she'd already phoned Arnold. It seems the Reverend Mother and all of us could have saved our time."

"What do you mean?"

"Joanna says she'd decided not to go back to the school anyway."

I waited.

"Apparently they've offered her a job at the pub and she says she's going to stay there and finish her A Levels by herself."

"What kind of job?"

"General chores, I suppose. The A Levels idea is quite impracticable, of course."

"What did she say about the man she'd been with? Is with?"

"When Arnold went to see her she wouldn't say anything about it at all. She just insisted it was only her business and that was it. He couldn't get a word out of her."

I thought about this. "Doesn't he want her to come home?" I said at last.

"Of course he does. He's really very worried in his own way. But he doesn't know what to do. He doesn't know what there is he can do, not at her age."

"Might moral danger or something come into it?"

"What?"

But even as I said the words it struck me that any attempt on Arnold's part to dispute the right of a nearly eighteen-year-old to her own life, whether or not it included a pub and a serviceman, would be an uphill task. And it wasn't only that. To have brought up the matter at all had given me a sense almost of generation disloyalty, of betraying the feeling of near fellowship I had begun to have with Joanna.

I said, "Joanna must miss her mother."

"She's never talked about her. Not to me anyway. Not that there was much opportunity. Her mother was the victim of the kind of passion you read about in novels which can argue that fifteen is practically grown up."

"Perhaps fifteen is."

"Perhaps it isn't," Cassie said quietly.

"Arnold wasn't quite as I'd imagined. I thought he might have a little moustache but he didn't. He was plumper, and he had more hair. There was the Rolex, of course. I didn't not like him."

"Joanna doesn't not like him. But I can't see them living together now in domestic amity. Since her mother isn't here to do it someone will have to do something."

"What can anyone do that Arnold can't? And there is the question of the soldier. I suppose sooner or later we're going to hear something about him."

"I don't want to hear about the soldier or anyone else," Cassie said, "until she's got her A Levels. That's only common sense for any girl." And that effectively was her last word on the subject.

When I went back to Hugh he told me that Alison was going to let them put up a horse shelter, and that he was going to be allowed to help feed Barbary.

*****

Developments moved quickly after that, largely engineered by Cassie. Arnold didn't go to Zurich but went again to Suffolk instead where he was deadlocked by a Joanna already working at the pub, saying she was going to go on working there, and wanting to make arrangements to collect things of hers both from home and the school. There appeared to be no sign of whoever it was who had previously been with her, and the glancing references James had made to abduction, challengeable influences and so forth seemed to come to nothing.

My own attitude gelled into a sort of ambivalence; one part of me was glad that she was showing herself independent of the decisions other people proposed to make for her and was going her own way, another part very well saw the objections.

It was Cassie who persuaded a somewhat dubious Peter that Joanna should come to stay with *them,* and afterwards went to see Mrs. Hallam, her friend as well as her headmistress.

By one of those coincidences that might make us exclaim in surprise but which in fact happen quite regularly, I also went to see Mrs. Hallam because she had said she wanted to see me.

She was a character in Whitethorn; fiftyish, widowed, with twin daughters at university. I thought of her predominantly as warm; wonderfully able to get on with people.

When I arrived she had been writing letters at the kitchen table and listening to the radio. On the table stood a tea pot and a milk bottle. Mrs. Carnaby, who also went to the cottage once a week to clean and was devoted to Mrs. Hallam, had once remarked quite without malice that if *she* bought Co-op milk at least she'd put it in a jug.

Mrs. Hallam turned off the radio and pulled up a chair for me. What she wanted me to do was talk to her discussion group about writing a novel.

"I couldn't. I couldn't do that. It would be like the blind leading the blind. *Mis*leading them, I shouldn't wonder, the way this one's going. I couldn't, possibly."

When she saw that I meant it she didn't persist. "First novels sometimes write themselves. But I don't think second ones very often do. Well, as soon as you feel you can talk to us. . . . Promise?"

"Yes," I said.

We had tea in her sitting room. She was no interior decorator. In this she reminded me of myself.

But one day I wanted to change, to overcome my lack of flair, and have a different home.

There was something else, too, that I wanted to change, sooner, as soon as I could, because I knew that at twenty-four a more or less adequate widow's pension from one's husband's firm was no way to live. I wanted to make money and do it by writing.

When I was leaving, Mrs. Hallam told me that Hugh's headmistress had remarked to her at some function or other she thought he would be fully settled in by Christmas.

What she told Cassie was that she would be delighted to have Joanna in her sixth form.

Only Joanna, approached by Cassie, said no.

*****

"My dear Roz, Cassie must have been mad!"

Alison and I had met for coffee at the Columbine, a café in Whitethorn where an elderly lady made cakes first thing in the morning and then put on a flowered apron and sold them without difficulty throughout the day. I liked macaroons. Hugh liked Battenburg, and Alison rarely exceeded a scone.

"Well the room's there," I said, "And —"

"It isn't a question of *housing*!" Alison's voice, without rising, conveyed an absolute of certainty. "Cassie proposes to take a teenage she-wolf under her husband's roof and you start talking about housing! Believe me, it wouldn't have been a question of that. I don't know much about this particular girl, of course, though we know something of what she's been up to. She's just a name to me. But I know the type. And surely so must you. For a start, all that awful bloom. It may be a wasting asset, but, my God, though, you don't want it under the same roof. And the chemicals working like yeast below the surface." Though she grimaced humorously at the words she seemed to mean them. "What on earth could Cassie have been thinking of? And her husband —"

"You could hardly call Peter a wolf."

"I was going to say within wincing distance of the dangerous forties."

"If she'd come to school here she would have had to have somewhere to live."

"So would Cassie!"

I smiled then. "Alison, what *are* you going on about? I think it's time you went home and did some more work. Your imagination is running away with you."

"It is time indeed. But let me tell you that leopards don't change their spots. And I wouldn't like to have watched Cassie coming a cropper over something she couldn't even see was there. By the way, that reminds me — for heaven's sake take that animal object of Hugh's out of your car window, it's too big, or the next thing you know you'll both be in hospital. And that's all he wants at the moment." Her tone for that had changed but then she returned to her theme. "At worst," she said, "Cassie could have had her marriage wrecked, your son could have been apprenticed to a life of —"

"My son isn't six!"

"Your house broken into by thug deserters on the run."

"With death rays?"

She laughed. "But I'm almost serious. The sort of thing Cassie was proposing could have led to practically anything. Things no one had ever thought of. It's the sort of idea that anyone with any sense would keep clear of."

But in the meantime Mrs. Hallam had taken a different view. She had written a note to Joanna telling her that if she cared to come one Sunday simply to discuss a program which might help her working on her own, she would be very welcome.

After some delay Joanna chose a weekend when I had promised to take Hugh to see my parents in Dorset. We returned for me to learn that she had half agreed by the end of the day to think about how much more practicable it would be to join Mrs. Hallam's sixth form for the few remaining months before her A Levels were due.

* * * * *

I went to meet her because Cassie was working. She was immediately recognizable to me as I walked towards her on the platform. Tall, the dark hair just touching the collar of her raincoat, which was off-white and belted. She had a sling handbag over one shoulder.

If I had expected any particular glow, any bloom resulting from her recent experiences, whatever these might have been, I would have been wrong. She was pale, and looked tired, and her face seemed thinner than in the photograph.

"I'm Joanna Patterson."

"I'm Roz." I hesitated. "I'm glad you've come." I said it simply because it was true.

She inclined her head very slightly, and half smiled. Her expression said, "Oh?," and I was reminded that though her story had become a part of my day-to-day life, *I* had had no story in which she might have felt involved. For her there was no relationship.

"It's a nice station," she said.

Her eyes were a sort of light brown, but very slightly flecked, with green was it? The word "tawny" came into my mind.

At the corner of the left eye was a tiny scar which, deep, minute, could have been made by the square tip of a relief nib. It showed more than it would have done had her skin been less smooth and unlined.

"Not much in the way of pretty tubs or whitewash. If they've won any prizes they've kept quiet about them."

"The booking office is pretty."

"At least it's here. Some of these stations are being closed down."

We walked together across the forecourt.

FOUR

In the days which immediately followed, that could have seemed that; no more, no story for us. We scarcely saw each other. Cassie and I had long ago come to a tacit and entirely amiable agreement that we should not make free with each other's parts of the house, and certainly Joanna gave no sign of wishing to breach the agreement. When we did encounter each other by chance our exchanges were about on a par with what we had had to say on the subject of the Whitethorn station.

She appeared to be working very hard both at school and at home, and somehow conveyed without any offense that the sole purpose of her stay was to finish with her exams, getting good grades at the first attempt.

For my part I worked on my book.

There was a small episode when she and I and Roger all more or less coincided outside the house, I returning from shopping, she going I didn't know where. Seeing us, Roger drove up and got out of his car. He was a fair, slight boy, with considerable charm, and a remarkably nice nature considering that he was the sole and absolute apple of his parents' eye, though Alison tried to pretend that he wasn't. He had grown a beard. His mothers' comment on this development was that it just made him look more like the anarchist he was — their views on life weren't always identical — but to me he looked the same pleasant young man who knew perfectly well where his next penny was coming from.

"Home for the weekend."

I introduced him to Joanna, and he must have heard something about her because he said, "How's it going? What are your subjects?"

"English and geography. Sociology."

"Sociology? I wouldn't be much use there. I've got a mass of English notes stacked away somewhere."

She smiled. "Oh?" she said without committing herself.

"What books are you doing?"

"Pope. Jane Austen."

"I'll see what I've got. Anyway, can I give you a lift?"

"I'm going to the library to do some work. I felt like the walk."

"Do you feel like the company?"

"Actually," she said, "I'm doing the work already. In my head."

"Oh come on, you're not going to turn into one of those girls who wear their work like a spare tire."

"I have already. For the moment."

"No Pope-ish elasticity?"

"None. Nor fire," she said, and they both laughed.

Then seeing that I was lost, she said, "We think we're quoting 'The Dunciad,' or at any rate I do. We might well be wrong. I'll go and find out. 'Bye, Roz."

Roger came and had a cup of coffee with me, sitting on the stool Hugh and I had painted yellow. Hugh was downstairs watching Cassie make a quiche for someone Peter had known in the navy. They had a lot of visitors.

When Hugh heard Roger he came upstairs and sat on his knee, which rather embarrassed Roger, but he was quite nice about it.

I later heard from Cassie that he had asked Joanna out for a drink but she hadn't gone.

*****

Then three things happened. Winter repented with a couple of days which would have done credit to September. Roger came home for the second weekend running, and Alison decided on a picnic, though in the event Roger didn't come on it.

The place chosen for the picnic was the common meandering picturesquely round an Elizabethan manor house about five miles from Whitethorn on the Wrayford road.

Chairs were set up, and the hock produced.

"I hope it won't be too dry for you," Alison said to Joanna in a quite friendly way.

Politely Joanna accepted the glass offered her, just, I felt, as she had accepted her invitation to the picnic.

Neutrally, merely a private observation, the words "well brought up" passed through my mind.

She was wearing a pale blue dress which buttoned right down without any gaping, and I thought, either she is good at wearing it, or it cost a lot of money.

On a whim Hugh had brought with him the toy panther that at one stage he had wanted hanging in the car, and as she sipped she made conversation to him about this.

"Well, Roz, how's the book going?" Alison said, handing me my glass.

"Better."

"Good. You know one day when I'm a dear little old lady —"

"Whatever makes you think you're going to be a dear little old lady?" Cassie said.

Alison started again. "One day, when I'm a dear little old lady and the fires are burning low and I begin to feel that what I need if not want is something restful, I may very well turn to a little light novel-writing. In which case I shall always have a picnic in all of my novels. They are so delightful. Don't you agree, Roz?"

"It might lend them a certain rarity value if you didn't."

"At any rate you're laying your plans in remarkably good time," Peter said.

She laughed, and acknowledged the comment graciously but without enlarging on its significance. We didn't really know how old she was. She wasn't evasive about this so much as simply uncommunicative.

"A certain amount of planning," she said now, "I do not object to in principle. Rather the reverse. And especially on a Sunday morning." It was a Sunday morning.

"Why?" Peter said. "On a Sunday morning, I mean?"

"Because I can see nothing advantageous at all," she replied, "in having two quite separate people turn up unplanned from out of the blue and want to take your son off to lunch with them."

"Is that what's happened?" Cassie was amused.

We already knew that Roger, after all, had gone off for lunch with a friend of his; but we hadn't yet been told the details.

"Yes; that's what's happened. And quite *half* the things I've brought with me, moreover, are what Roger said would help to keep him happy if — I quote — he was to mix it with mole-hills and mosquitos. Though really I cannot help feeling that on even such a beautiful weekend as this the mosquitos are an exaggeration."

Alison gave Peter her "I ask you" look.

"Well, never mind him," Peter said at this. "It's nice for us."

And it really was.

With the weather and the wine, the smoked trout, Alison's pâté, each person's favorite cheese, gruyère for me, and Joanna chose this too, each person's favorite fruit — it was nice.

Not that it was Hugh's kind of picnic. He would have preferred banana sandwiches under the trees in the children's playground; he didn't seem to be hungry, and he didn't particularly want to sit up at the table.

Alison's picnics had a rather formal, organized quality about them, and involved cutlery, and "great delicacies." Hugh didn't want cold soup, for all that it was undoubtedly a great delicacy, and he didn't want his napkin. He quite soon decamped to the grass, where he played with his panther and some marbles.

Alison smiled upon this because Hugh was a favorite of hers, but as a general rule she didn't very much like anything she felt to be a disruptive occurrence outside her own arranged pattern — not even on a picnic. She certainly hadn't very much liked the fact that Roger should have taken off unexpectedly that morning to have lunch somewhere else.

"*Two* of them," she said, as she took a hard-boiled egg from one of her picnic baskets and put it on a small blue picnic plate, where it began to roll; quickly she subdued the rolling. If there was one thing that would have been totally unacceptable to her, it was a shelly mess. "There, try him with an egg." She handed the plate to me. "You're the maternal one."

"I'm thirsty," Hugh said. I gave him some orange juice, and began to shell the egg.

"The girl was all right, as far as it went," Alison was saying. "Pretty little thing. Vicar's daughter, I think he said. I've seen *them* looking like something in an outsize flower pot. But the trouble with all these vicars' families when it comes to lunch is that there's never anyone there who can cook. I murmured as much in Roger's ear. I don't really *know,* of course, if a fatted calf takes much cooking; not that I think he's seen her more than about twice, but that certainly doesn't have to make any difference these days. To say the girls are in a hurry is to understate your case."

Joanna stroked the panther.

"As the mother of a son I can aver it categorically. Well, anyway, he was busy dithering about the invitation — I'll say one thing for Roger, he's got a kind heart — when the other one turned up."

"What other one?" Cassie said.

"The one Roger met at a party. Looked like a tramp. Trust Roger to go to a party and emerge bosom friends with the one called Bill who looks like a tramp. That's what a good school's done for him. Bill *Moon,* I believe he said, some such improbable name. Comes from Wapping. Not that Roger would mind if he came from Dartmoor."

"What's Dartmoor?" Hugh glanced up.

"Prison. Top security." Alison always answered Hugh's questions with brisk veracity. "Been at sea all his life. Forty-five if he's a day now."

"What kind of at sea?" Peter asked. I had once heard Peter remark that he might have considered staying in the navy if he hadn't wanted to come home to Cassie more. The thought occurred to me that their recent visitor could have stirred up some nostalgia.

"Most kinds, I shouldn't wonder," Alison said. "Tramp or not, though, his car was ship shape, if you'll forgive the expression. I'll say that for him. The bundles in the back were a model of neatness. And he did know what he wanted. According to Roger, too, he seems to have saved up a sizable amount of cash."

"What does he want?" Peter said.

"His own boat for selling holidays abroad."

"Give me fishing any time," said James.

"Mr. Moon's idea," Alison continued, "was to take Roger over to Stainton to look at something there with him. Stainton," Alison explained to Joanna, "is our nearest seaside — quite a center for messing about in boats."

"So in the end," Cassie said, "did this Bill go off to the vicarage too?"

"No, not on your life. Not Bill. He put it to them that what he fancied was bacon and eggs, having been up since five without any breakfast, so Roger went to the vicarage, and he went to the Crown and Horseshoes; what he really fancied at the Crown and Horseshoes, though, I believe we can all imagine."

Alison adjusted an expensive earring, and leaned back slightly in her chair.

"The sun, the sun," she said after a pause. "The lovely sun." She used the trick of infusing irony even into remarks she meant, especially if they revealed anything about her, any temperamental inclination or disinclination, which she intellectually half-disowned. The winter sun, though, was presumably an impeccable leaning even for an intellectual. "They should have given that horse a patio while they were about it."

"What horse?" Joanna said, and Hugh looked up. At which James, having mildly crushed his napkin and put it aside, and taken off his spectacles, told her the story of Barbary.

"Who looks after him?"

"Oh, his owners look after him. Rather cautiously, I might say. But his every material need is attended to. It's his social life is a bit thin."

"We were hoping," said Alison, "to interest Roger. But it has not proved one of his priorities."

James said, "Those come and go. Have their exits and their entrances."

Alison nodded. "And each girl in her time plays many cards."

I said to Joanna, "The entire family seems set on proving how unintimidated they are by an English student." She gave me quick smile.

"Would they let me ride him?" she said to Alison.

"Do you ride?"

"Since I was three."

For a moment I wondered if Alison was going to say something like "a girl of many parts" but she didn't. How far the picture she had been painting of Roger had been aimed at Joanna, consciously or unconsciously, I wasn't sure. But clearly she seemed to have no objection to a blossoming relationship with a horse. "I should think they'd be delighted," she said. "I'll certainly ask them."

Cassie remarked that they really ought to change Barbary. And James said that that would be a definitive statement of having made a mistake. "Besides, changes aren't always for the best. He's a magnificent animal."

We were still sitting up at the table almost, it occurred to me, as if in expectation of a bill, and it was then that Alison suggested a walk.

"James is quite right," she said, as we passed the manor house which was central to the common where we had been picnicking. "About changes. It's often as well to leave things as they are. I personally lament, for example, the passing of the squirearchy." She spoke in her characteristic half-ironic tone. "Take most of these beautiful houses now. God knows who's in them. Whereas once —"

James put in, "We can imagine what Roger would say to that."

"Roger says so many things. I will not, however, even for Roger — even for displaying the absence of all class consciousness in me — exclaim sycophantically over the presence of dustmen in what were once wonderful homes."

Joanna and I were walking side by side. It was then that she turned to me so that our eyes met, the words only for me, and murmured of Alison, "Can't stand snobbery or dustmen." I think it was the first time I saw the smile that was almost a laugh, heard the small sound of breath.

At home she said, "Roz, you won't let Mrs. Elliott forget about Barbary, will you?"

"No, I won't."

"How old is Mrs. Elliott?"

I shrugged.

"She talks a lot. I wonder if she's ever been happy. I mean, ecstatically happy."

*****

Mrs. Carnaby was the first to discover them. "That child," she said, "has got spots."

And he had. Moreover, from the wealth of her experiences she knew what they were. "The little flat pinky ones and snuffly with it," she said. "You can always tell. And it's about. My neighbor's boy's down with it. The one who does conjuring. Keep him indoors a few days and he'll be as right as rain."

Shortly afterwards Joanna came upstairs. "Can I see Hugh a minute?"

"He's got German measles."

"Yes, I know."

"Well, do you want —"

When I didn't ask her in she looked at me a moment, then she said, merely stating it as a fact, "I'm not pregnant."

"No, but —" I could have added that I had never thought she would be. Only she had taken me by surprise.

She went on, still looking directly at me, "Absolutely not. It's absolutely *the* last thing I'd have wanted out of it. With Steve. It was going to be just something different, really. When you've been at the same school for three years, any school, well —" She stopped, and when she spoke again it was to say, "I'm going to the book shop.

There's something I need to get hold of. Mrs. Hallam's kind, but their sociology doesn't exist. Odd, *I'd have thought,* when you think it's an all girls' school. We had quite a strong group. Anyway, I was going to get Danek's *Book of Horses* for Hugh. If he hasn't got it already."

"He hasn't," I said, trying not to think exclusively about what she had just said earlier. "He'd love it. Anything about horses. He's asleep at the moment. But do you want German measles?"

"Not particularly. Not at this precise moment. Only you can't just creep through life always being afraid of things, can you? Still, if he's asleep. . . . I'll get the book for him. I always loved it. The drawings are marvelous."

As it happened she had to order the book and it was several days before she brought it up to him. I could hear them talking in his room.

"That one looks a bit like Barbary," he said. "Will you really ride him? Barbary, I mean."

"Not at first. I'll talk to him first. Horses have to get to like you. Besides, Cassie says I've got to get my riding hat or she'll veto the whole thing. She could, too. He belongs to one of her pupils."

"What's veto?" Hugh said.

I didn't hear her answer to this but it made him laugh.

He was back at school when really I saw her again. I was going out on my way to collect him.

She came up to me. "Roz, do you know what?" she said. "Mrs. Hallam has fixed it for me to sit in on a juvenile court. I don't know how, but she has. She seems able to fix anything."

"Even you."

For the second time our eyes met in a personal way, as they had done on the picnic; briefly, we seemed to hold each other's gaze. Then, as if quite on the spur of the moment, she said, "You come. It would be all right. Do, Roz. It will really be interesting."

The pleasure I felt at this, as I understand better now than I did at the time, was more than simple pleasure. It had to do, I think, with suddenly having escaped, after all, the nothing, the no relationship with her.

"Will you come?"

"All right. If Mrs. Hallam can organize it. And if you'll promise me just one thing."

"It's possible," she said, and laughed.

"That you won't tell me it would make good copy."

FIVE

Mrs. Hallam arranged everything perfectly. We were expected and shown to unobtrusive seats where we could have been any kind of official.

The courtroom reminded me more of a small library than anything to do with the law. It had bookshelves round the walls, and the same atmosphere of quiet, of seclusion almost, of being withdrawn from the world.

There was a characteristic smell of antiseptic polish. The lights hung down stiffly from the ceiling, each a white ball at the end of a rod. From out of the high windows there was just the sky to be seen. Winter was decisively back and it was a sky dark and cold with rain clouds. Three magistrates came in and we all stood while they arranged themselves in their seats.

Joanna glanced at me.

A policewoman appeared with a boy.

Though it was true that the three chairs behind the magistrates' table did appear rather imposing, with their tall, monogrammed blue leather backs, the setting on the whole was clearly meant not to alarm nor even to awe but simply to underline the character of the proceedings, which weren't essentially penal.

The first two cases were both boys, I recall without much definition, both with anxious mothers, both in trouble for offensive weapons, I think it was. The first boy wore glasses, somehow to my surprise.

Of the three magistrates, two were men. The older one, the chairman, was a thick-set, breezy sort of man who could easily have been, for instance, a sea captain, or a certain type of professional soldier. He was the one who was to do most of the talking.

When he had begun, Joanna, I suppose feeling that any further conversation on our part would be inappropriate, wrote a note on her pad and showed it to me. It read: "Name your sociology question — I'll work this in by hook or by crook."

I smiled.

Looking round me I found the windows reminded me of Alison's studio, and in some odd way this very fact underlined the unfamiliarity of my surroundings — surroundings where I was solely because Joanna had suggested it.

Though I was entirely aware of her attractiveness, I think at that stage I had no consciousness of a sexual feeling starting up between us. I wouldn't, then, have looked for it. But it seems to me now that it must have been there almost from the beginning. I know as we sat together in that courtroom I was intensely conscious of her nearness.

Following the second boy the next case to be heard was a girl of about fifteen, a Care and Protection case. She was in a blue corduroy dress. She had untidy, unevenly bleached hair, a lot of make-up and a curiously gentle face, I thought. She was without stockings; her shoes were black, and cheap, with very high heels.

She sat seeming quite passive while there was some paper shuffling and a little mild conferring among the magistrates.

Joanna wrote another note: "She's nice."

The chairman began in a blunt, vigorous voice to the girl seated before him. "Joyce, now tell me — do you go to church?"

The girl didn't seem to expect the question; anyway, she said "no" as if it had surprised her, then added, "I did."

"Don't you think if you'd kept on going you might not be here before us today?"

There was no reply.

He waited for his words to sink in. "Did you have your father's permission to be courting this young man" — he looked at his papers — "this young man, Ian Kemp?"

"No." She hesitated. "He wouldn't have given it."

"Did you think one day you were going to marry him?"

"I don't know."

I felt Joanna change her position.

The chairman didn't press his point. "Perhaps," he said to the woman I took to be the probation officer, "you'd tell us all about this."

When she had complied, he said, his tone still blunt, but not unkind, "Have you had sexual relations with other boys?"

It was at this point I became aware that something of Joanna's early positive attitude to the proceedings was beginning to slip away, was changing gradually to a kind of silent dissent. Though the physical means by which she could give expression to this were limited, I could feel it happening at my side, the dissent, it seemed to me, growing in her almost like something tangible.

"Joyce, I want you to listen very carefully to what I'm going to say." The chairman sipped from his glass of water. The tone he was using now was clearly the one he used for those known to have been causing trouble, but to whom he was prepared to give every chance. *Girls.* It was the voice of a man to a girl — straight from the shoulder but all the same less hard hitting than it had been in the case of the boys, different in essence.

I looked at Joanna's face.

"There's altogether too much sitting on the fence by people like me these days," the chairman went on. "So I'm going to come right out into the open and say to you that what you've done is wrong. You may have heard a lot of silly talk going about; I expect you have. It suits some people to see that you should. But believe me, purity and chastity for a girl can never be out of date. What she does with her body is what she does with herself. It should be sacred to her."

Joanna was once more writing something.

The chairman then seemed to become very conversational. He pushed back his chair a little, and faced the girl regardingly. Because his voice was now lower I couldn't quite hear what he was saying until his tone rose again on — "What I hope is going to happen to you is that you're going to grow up, and soon find the right boy, not one who can never be any good to you, and who breaks the law, and just leaves you to get on with it, but the *right* one, and you're going to get married, and you're going to be responsible for his happiness, and he's going to be responsible for yours. And what's more, he's going to give you a guarantee, a contract."

I looked at Joanna's note. "This is the fifties!!"

"Because I don't mind telling you," the chairman was continuing, "that if any of my business friends started behaving the way some of you girls behave, I'd think he was a bit soft in the head. Nothing written down. No protection of any sort —"

"Unilateral disarmament, in fact," the younger man said. "Do you understand what that means?"

"No," the girl said.

"It means giving the other chap every advantage."

The woman magistrate then lent her agreement to this general proposition, but the chairman hadn't finished, though the words that he spoke, doubtless having been spoken so many times before, began to seem as though they had some effortless, gliding quality about them; a little like ice-hockey pucks, I thought, covering a neat, familiar course over smooth and unresisting ice. (Tom had liked ice hockey, had taken me to the odd match after we were married.)

"Now you and me and her and him and the next chap, all of us, that's *society*. The rough-necks coming into this court-room can do damage to society with their knives and their coshes and the rest of it — but, believe me, no more than *you* can do by behaving badly as a woman. We need you to behave well." He regarded the girl. "Have pride in yourself as a woman. Be able to respect yourself for what you are. Don't throw yourself away. You're for better things than that —" He had forgotten her name, and glanced down at his papers for it. "— Joyce," he said. "Now what I want you to promise me for the future is that you're going to choose wisely when it comes to young men."

"And preferably once," the younger man said.

I don't know whether he really meant that or whether it was a little off-the-cuff alliteration that he couldn't resist, but it resulted in Joanna's final note, which read, "Can't we go now?"

We delayed a little longer for appearances' sake, but outside on the pavement she could hardly wait to exclaim, "It was awful! Roz, it was really awful! I couldn't bear it. What did they think they were doing to that girl? They seemed to be trying to tie her up hands and feet for the rest of her life. I really couldn't bear it. I wanted to go and be with her and undo the knots they were tying up. Didn't *you* want to?"

"I don't think even Mrs. Hallam could have organized that for us."

"I'm sorry about Mrs. Hallam, but I just couldn't stay there with them."

Looking at her I could see how impassioned she felt; how much more there was still to be said.

"Is there anywhere we could go?" she asked. "I don't want to go back to the house yet."

I glanced at my watch. "In ten minutes," I said, "the Johnny Onion will be open."

*****

The Johnny Onion was a basement wine bar in Whitethorn owned by a Frenchman who, having originally come to England to sell onions, had married an

English widow, and settled here. The place had been intentionally given a "French" atmosphere, and was in fact rather reminiscent of a French café. The tables were covered with bright blue, white and red cloths, and the frilly curtains had patterns with such symbols as the *Loterie Nationale,* the Metro and garret windows with shutters and flower pots. There were pretty little French flags on the tables, and among the lines of bottles were further touches here and there of France — a Gauloise packet, a silver miniature of a Caravelle, a vegetable mill.

There was a faint smell of butter and herbs. Although it was really a wine bar, Johnny himself did a little cooking by arrangement. He was a small, pointed man who wore a beret as part of the job, and spoke cockney English with a French accent.

We were the first to arrive and he took us to a corner table with comfortable, upholstered benches at right angles to each other — and brought us our drinks himself.

The bar was gratefully warm, the lighting pinkish and very dim. It could have been made for talking.

Joanna hung her raincoat round her shoulders. She had on a rather sober sweater and skirt although Mrs. Hallam, her aim characteristically to be helpful and not to exact conformity, had waived school uniform on the ground that it would be for so short a time.

The dark wool wonderfully set off her heightened color, a glow, so absent when she had first arrived in Whitethorn, which circumstances had now connived at — not just a cold wind, but a mood of protest that had persisted throughout our walk from the court.

She played a moment in silence with her glass as if making some conscious effort now to adjust her mood.

The Frenchman's gaze lingered on her.

Perhaps it could have been an intimation to me of the nature of what was to come that, also looking at her — in my case without objectivity and with no tinge of envy — what I felt was something like pure sensual pleasure.

I said, "I wonder what Mrs. Hallam would say if she saw us."

Joanna laughed. "Not very much. We'll hardly go to hell on the house white."

"Let alone the house white with soda?"

She went on, suddenly serious, "But, anyway, Mrs. Hallam understands that I'm not really back at school. Not properly. I couldn't do that. It happened at the half term. I didn't plan it to happen, Roz. I mean about leaving school. And it was nothing to do with the Reverend Mother. It just happened. It was like, oh, I don't know, a curtain being drawn across. Something of the sort. The absolute finish of that bit. Only Mrs. Hallam made me see it might be rather a waste just to throw away all the A Level work. Not that I really know what good it will be to me. Whether I'll ever really need it."

I waited, and she continued. "Mrs. Hallam's sixth form's great. But the way I feel seems to cover everything. I don't want school friends any more."

"Cassie says you get on very well with them."

"I wouldn't go to Cassie's school and not get on with people. Would I? Not the way Cassie and Peter have been. But I can't be a schoolgirl any more. Roz, can you understand that?"

"Yes." She smiled at me, and I added, "You'll need the A Levels for University." When she smiled, there was something generous about her mouth, a little like Cassie's, I thought, though there was no blood relationship between them.

"I'm not sure about University. I'm not sure now about anything that's going to last a long time. Cassie wants me to apply for a place. I won't, though. I'll wait and see what happens. I don't know what I want to do. I'll just get three grade As and then I'll make up my mind nearer the time. With that, someone, somewhere, would accept me."

"Only three grade As?"

"Well, maybe two As and a B. And I've got a nice flexible group of subjects. Geography can go either way. I mean arts or science."

"Is that why you chose it?"

"Not really. I think I chose it to have some idea at any given time where my parents were." She drank some of her wine. Differently from at the picnic. Less formally. "My father's in Singapore. I had a letter from him today. I'm sorry I bothered my father. We don't really understand each other. But he didn't just go off to Zurich though, did he?"

"No. No, he didn't."

"But that girl this morning, Roz, there didn't seem to be any sign of her parents. She didn't seem to have anyone of her own. And as for the woman magistrate — she was worse than useless. I felt ashamed of her. Ashamed because she was a woman. I thought the girl needed someone to stand up for her."

"Only to say what?"

"Even if we're not very good at it to start with we can't go through life on a lead. It's better to mess things up than that. We can't weigh out relationships as if they were something in a sweet shop. Roz, can we?"

"No."

"And the man who kept on talking, the chairman one, well, there he was in the middle with his real leather chair and the crests and all the rest of it, and the awful thing is he might have been going to convince that nice girl he was right, she *should* live her life all frightened and small and calculating everything. He was put up there as sort of God, Father, Authority. She just might have ended up believing him. I so wanted to argue I had to come out."

"Well, they wouldn't have let you."

"No, I know. And that's what was so unfair. I mean, it's different with someone like Alison, say. She talks all the time but you could argue with her if you wanted to."

"And Alison doesn't mean half of what she says, anyway. She does it to entertain, to provoke, to create a little interest."

Joanna laughed. "And you don't have to take any notice if you don't want to. She probably ought to have been an actress. No, a producer. She likes to manage people, doesn't she? Anyway, a different life. So that she didn't have to worry about little things like who was going to win her son. Not that he isn't quite nice. It *was* 'The Dunciad,' by the way."

"Was it?"

"You know, Pope would never have agreed with that chairman!"

The Frenchman returned and inquired if we were all right. I had another glass of wine, but Joanna refused.

I said, "I think the girl, Joy —"

"Joyce."

"Joyce. I think Joyce seemed a bit of a natural victim. I think it would have been very easy to have her thrown to the wolves. I doubt she has your powers of organization."

"*Me?*" Joanna exclaimed. She shook her head, so that the hair fell forward a little. "I came *completely* unstuck." She paused. "Zero for organization as it turned out. But I'm not going to live the rest of my life as though I daren't put one foot before the other. I'm not going to live it at all like that. Just because things didn't quite work out the first time."

There was a moment's silence. She had finished her wine, and after a slight hesitation she took a sip of mine. "It's nicer without the soda," she said. "Roz, do you know why I wanted that week with Steve? I've never tried to explain to anyone else. I'm not sure I've ever tried to explain it to me."

I wanted her to go on. But I didn't want overtly to encourage. I didn't say anything because I didn't know what to say that mightn't be wrong.

"I met him on the train going back to school at the beginning of the term. He was in the same carriage. I was with Pauline," she said. "She was my friend, at school. Well, she still is my friend. But about Steve. He's stationed at a camp near the school. And the thing about him was, he knew almost at once what he wanted was me, for the time being. And he was going to get it if he could. He was very good at that. He thought of all sorts of ways for getting in touch with me. And *he* wasn't a business man. And he'd been married, and he didn't ever want to be again, and I thought he would be a kind of experience. Different from anything I'd come up against before." She looked at me. "And he was a different experience. As a matter of fact, one I could have done without. But it didn't really matter. It started me off on not being a schoolgirl."

"I thought you might have been with a wine baron."

Joanna laughed. "Why a wine baron?"

"I don't know. It just somehow seemed less worrying than a lot of things."

"And richer?" She returned to playing with her glass. "It's funny, but my mother was engaged to a wine importer before she met my father." The glass was twirled round and returned to its place on the table. Her nails, I noted in a kind of parenthesis, were rather short, and carefully filed; the fingers met round the glass. "You know, Roz, *she* wanted to slip her lead. Only really she left it a bit late." Then she added, as though from some kind of compulsive loyalty, "I could have gone with her. But I'd just have been part of the lead. Wouldn't I? I'll visit her again. Later. Sometime later."

"I don't think you would be part of anyone's lead," I said, meaning it.

But she didn't want to talk about this any more. Clearly to change the subject she said, "I wonder if Mrs. Hallam's life has been strewn with lovers."

"That's really something I don't know about Mrs. Hallam."

"I'm sure it has. I wonder if she's so nice because she's had lots of lovers or she's had lots of lovers because she's so nice. Tell me something, Roz. Do you think there's a special kind of morality for sex?"

"No."

"We were talking about it at one of her discussion groups. Another thing. Mrs. Hallam thinks there is such a thing as pure morality. I mean, sort of existing in its own right. But I don't think I do. I think morality is really a question of what you make happen. Don't you? Don't you think it is?"

"Yes, I think I do. I think I agree with you. I think I'd go further. I think it's mostly a question of being reasonable."

"Oh, good. Oh, good, Roz. I'm glad you think so, too." Then she said, "You know, it's very funny," as she looked at me, her look direct, "but I seem to have waited until I was in a place that was half dark before I really began to see you. I mean I could have said that you had light hair, and grayish eyes —" she smiled. "At least I think I could have said they were grayish. But now I'm suddenly seeing you, Roz."

"Is that good or bad?"

"It's good. Of course it's good. It's 'Roz, my friend' good. Don't you think so?"

"Of course I do."

There was a silence again between us.

To analyze just what I felt would have been difficult then and isn't easy now. But somewhere in the feeling of gladness — and this at a time when I had over many months been deliberately turning away from any kind of intimacy with another person, except for Hugh — was a trace almost of triumph, of success. I can't explain it exactly, but the Joanna on the platform at Whitethorn station had now become this Joanna.

She was saying, "And you're going to talk about writing novels to one of the discussion groups, aren't you? When you're ready. I shall be very proud. What is the book you're writing now about, Roz?"

"Oh, Joanna. I don't know. I don't think you can ask that. I think it's about not falling in love. But I don't think of it as being *about* anything. I think of it as being. Of wanting to make it what I want it to *be*."

"Yes. I see what you mean. I think I do. 'About' is just the getting born bit for a book. It was a silly question to ask. When will I be able to read it? Will you have finished by Christmas?"

"Not by Christmas. But perhaps not too long afterwards. So it should be out by the end of next year."

"Aren't we both busy!" Joanna thought about this for a moment. "The end of next year. I wonder what we'll both be doing by the end of next year." She continued thinking to herself, and I offered her my glass. She sipped from it. Then she said, "I wonder if I *can* say this. But I will, anyway. Now that we're friends. Do you think by the end of next year you will be thinking of perhaps getting married again?"

She was quick to note my silence, and said, not waiting for a reply, "I seem to be asking all the wrong questions." So that, because of all that she had said to me, in not answering her question, I had a sense of ungenerosity. But I couldn't. It was something I didn't want to talk about still, to her, or to anyone else. Perhaps now, though, I should have thought "even to her."

"One day?" Joanna said. "Maybe one day."

As we prepared to leave the bar she took hold of my hand. In a friendly way. In a consoling way. I didn't know. But it was nice. The Frenchman picked up our glasses. "Au revoir, madame, mademoiselle," he said. "À beintôt."

The wind outside was still cold.

SIX

The next day it was my turn to have a letter. Oddly a continuation of the Gallic connection.

Aged fifteen and in the fourth form I had become the pen-friend, the "*marraine*" as he somewhat quaintly called it, of a Free French sailor fighting with de Gaulle. The scheme had been sponsored by my French teacher, partly in the interests of allied solidarity, but more, I suspect, in the interest of his pupils' French. In my case this didn't work out too well. Yves was an interpreter whose English was excellent and which he was set on making perfect.

Still, we enjoyed our correspondence, more perhaps than our meetings, which occurred when he had leave, and the contact had persisted in a spasmodic sort of way after the war.

When he was demobilized he had returned to his firm in Paris, stamp dealers I think they were, or it might have been coins; anyhow, his work brought him to London now and again for a couple of days and we usually met. The firm had a flat in Westminster which I had been to a few times, and twice he had stayed with us, though not at Whitethorn. I had seen him only once since Tom's death.

I suppose it is absurd to talk about such a thing as a typical Frenchman but few people I imagine would have thought of Yves as this. He was tall and blond and a teetotaler — very much one on his own.

His latest letter said that he would be in London shortly, and that he had arranged two tickets for the House of Commons — where he had never been — for the 17th. And that if I had nothing better to do, perhaps I would like to go with him and have supper afterwards.

I thought about it.

The cold weather remained but now it had become frosty with a brilliant sun and, having to go to the bank, I decided to walk to Whitethorn by the stream.

I hadn't gone far when I saw Joanna coming towards me. "I've been to see Barbary," she said. "He really is marvelous. I'm going to ride him round the field this weekend. Roz, I was going to ask you. Can Hugh come and watch?"

"Yes. But if you don't let him into the field."

"Oh?" She sounded surprised. "Why?"

"Because you can't trust a five-year-old. Any moment he could get excited and be under your feet."

"Oh. Oh, yes, I see." She nodded. "I hadn't thought of that. Roz, I must go. I've got some books to pick up. We're having a week of tests. Beginning today." She kissed my cheek. "See you."

"See you," I said.

It was early and the bank wasn't yet busy. The door of the room James had as an office was open and I could see him on the small pair of steps he used for the purpose of selecting high-up ledgers; he was studying the lettering on the back of one of them.

Aware of my presence, he descended carefully, rather conscious of his dignity.

"Good morning, Mrs. Taylor," he said, as if our relations were formal, but he smiled. He took off his spectacles.

Probably if I had been to lose touch with the Elliotts, one of the things I would have remembered most clearly about him would have been the way that, when thinking or attending, he sometimes did take off his spectacles — which, in contrast to Alison's, were a slender gold. Sometimes he covered his eyes a moment with his hands. I shouldn't think anyone seeing him do this could ever have imagined him capable for an instant of any act which was at all hasty or ill-considered. Or for that matter lacking in dignity.

On the whole Whitethorn was rather pleased to have him. (It was rather pleased, anyway, to have so superior a bank.) Everyone was sure he could have done much bigger things than banking — if he hadn't happened to like country life, and if he hadn't happened to have a rich wife. Certainly he always looked very at ease in his bank.

"We're expecting Roger home again this weekend," he said, in the course of making conversation to me. "It's becoming quite a habit. Alison's delighted, naturally.

Except that there's some talk of that Moon fellow coming, too. The yacht he's got his eye on in Stainton is still very much in the air, I gather. I only hope he doesn't want to borrow any money from me. I'd have no hesitation at all in turning the idea down flat, Roger or no Roger. Second-hand yachts aren't up my street. Still, if they're going to Stainton they can take a good look at the hut. Save me a job."

What he spoke of as the hut was in reality more a rather luxurious wooden chalet on the sandy front at Stainton which they used quite often in the summer.

"I always like to give it the once-over before Christmas," James was saying, "check for wrack and ruin, you know, and again before the spring. Talking of Christmas, will you be visiting Swanage?"

"No," I said. "Not actually at Christmas. My parents are going to an aunt of mine who's been rather ill. Hugh and I will go down there for the New Year."

"Good," he said amiably. "Nice time of the year for Dorset. By the way, I saw that young lady of Cassie's with the horse this morning. They seemed to be getting on like a house on fire. Quite characters, both of them." He laughed.

The actuality of Joanna as opposed to the idea of her had made its impact.

"Well — what can I do for you, Mrs. Taylor?" he said then.

The "Mrs. Taylor" was only half a pleasantry intended to be a little amusing, and was half because he was, as he might have put it, on duty.

He accorded me the privileged treatment as a neighbor of cashing my cheque himself.

Outside the bank the morning traffic flashed and shone in the brilliant sunlight.

Someone was moving empty beer barrels over the cobblestones of the Crown and Horseshoes' courtyard opposite. It turned out to be Mrs. Carnaby's father.

In coming to live with his daughter, Mrs. Carnaby's father had profited from her strong sense of Christian duty without at all subscribing to anything similar himself; although he was eighty almost, and had a "heart," he was an unrepentant atheist. Nothing anemic like an agnostic, as Roger had once pointed out, but a full-blooded, thorough-going atheist. This, and his beer drinking, I suppose were the two main thorns in Mrs. Carnaby's flesh with regard to him, though there were many others.

These others didn't surprise her. In general she regarded men as trials you had to be "up to," which I believe I mentioned before — it was such a central part of her philosophy. Certainly she saw her father as no exception.

But he had an octogenarian determination to go his own way which would have done credit to a teenager, and which regularly proved something of a match for her.

I fluctuated as to whose side I was on.

About to cross the road now to speak to him, I heard a familiar voice behind me say, "You've beaten me to it. Hang on a minute, Roz, and I'll give you a lift back."

It was Peter. I turned round and saw him at the entrance to the bank.

After he had cashed his cheque we went together to his car and got in. "What are you doing home, anyway?" I said.

"Day off for Christmas shopping. That's the theory of the thing."

He pulled out into the traffic. He was a statistician for a drug firm and, with his serious, even cerebral look, this wasn't difficult to believe though, unlike Yves, a part of his heart had been left at sea. It passed through my mind that almost any yacht would have been up his street.

"Peter, are you doing anything on the 17th?"

"Firm's dinner. Why?"

"Oh, it's not important. I was just thinking I might go to London. Yves Martin's here with the belated whim to visit the House of Commons. Have you ever been?"

"Ages ago. Have you?"

"No, but it can wait. It doesn't matter."

"Well, Mrs. Carnaby would pick Hugh up for you if you wanted to go."

"Yes. Only it's the evening. Mrs. Carnaby isn't much of an evening sitter."

Peter moved into top gear.

"I expect Joanna would," he said. "She won't have gone by then."

"Gone?" I glanced at him. "Where is she going?"

"To stay with Arnold for a day or two. It's her birthday on the twenty —" He paused. "Twenty-first, I think. Then she was going to spend Christmas with some school friend. But she seems to have changed her mind about that."

Why, I wondered. I said, "What's her father doing?"

"Going to Kuwait. That chap certainly likes a change of scene."

"Perhaps she does, too. Perhaps it's something she does get from him."

"Oh, she's her mother's daughter. Anyway, she's coming back on Christmas Eve. Just in time for Mrs. Hallam's 'Entertainment.' If she's unlucky. You know, Roz, I sometimes feel as Christmas bears down on us that human ideals are a bit too much for human beings."

"I think I've always felt it."

"My parents are coming. And my brother and his wife. And at a rough count I'd say half the people we've ever known. Have you got any spare blankets? Oh, and by the way, Cassie's going to ask you if Joanna could have your spare room. Just over the holiday period. We could make up some kind of a bed for her. Would that be all right?"

"Yes," I said. "Of course it would."

*****

At the House of Commons Yves greeted me with a handshake — as always in our purely friendly relationship.

Apart from the big things, the architecture, the sheer age and history of the place, I found the details, particularly the contemporary details, of interest because of what in sum total they amounted to: the current government of a country.

The inside of the building reminded me somewhat of the glossy pictures used to advertise luxury liners. This was particularly true, I thought, of the empty writing room.

People had their umbrellas taken from them by a large, polite man in uniform before they were let into the public gallery of the debating chamber.

The chamber felt airless despite the air conditioning, and the microphones were confusing since Members talking on the floor of the House seemed to be lodged somewhere in the roof, so that from time to time Yves asked me what had been said.

The M.P.s looked shabbier and unhealthier than I had expected. One or two of them appeared to be dozing.

The debate was on fish. It didn't retain our interest indefinitely.

As we walked down Whitehall on our way to the block owned by Yves' firm we talked about fish recipes and then about the auction which had brought him to London. After that we looked for things to say. It had always seemed strange to me how on paper over the years we had found plenty to discuss of mutual interest, but how when we were together this was different.

The flat combined careful interior decoration with the characterlessness of somewhere that has never belonged to anyone in particular. On a small shelf provided for it was a glass ornament. Perhaps "ornament" isn't the right word but it's what I thought of it as being. I didn't like it, though it was beautifully and skillfully made. It was of tulips that had wilted so that they stooped grotesquely round the side of their vase like pecking ostriches or cranes. An electric fire had been recessed elegantly into the wall. Yves turned on two of the bars. The chairs had a kind of chic, but were not very comfortable.

I had written to him that I didn't want anything to eat, only coffee, and he had compromised by making his own onion soup. As he took off his pullover to put the finishing touches to this he said, "Do you remember when you knitted me a pullover? I still have it at home somewhere."

Actually I had never knitted him or anyone else anything. I had tried long ago once to learn without much success but the desire had never been very great and in the end it had come to nothing. What had happened with Yves was that in the first flush of my *marraine* duties I had spared some of my own clothing coupons and sent him the ensuing purchase. But somehow I couldn't be bothered to go into all that at this late stage.

Faintly from somewhere in the block came the sound of a radio. Though I couldn't hear the words I recognized the tune. By the merest chance a woman was singing "Long Ago and Far Away."

He brought the soup. He was wearing a gray silk shirt and had loosened his tie so that it was twisted a little too far to one side. It gave him a rather domestic look. He handed me the bowl of Parmesan he had grated.

It was when it came to the coffee that he passed mine to me over my shoulder, standing behind me, and bending close, so that his face was against mine. His hands then were on my elbows, and the fingers tightened.

Something about his new, unexpected move irritated me. I had the feeling that it had been done often before and that now it was my turn. My immediate wish was to sidestep it so that there could be no misunderstanding.

His next move was to turn my face to his and kiss my mouth. I avoided a further kiss.

"Yves," I said, drinking my coffee rather quickly, "I must go. I have a baby-sitter waiting for me at home."

He didn't argue. He phoned for a taxi to take me to the station, and we talked civilly while we waited for it to arrive, though not without some awkwardness on my part at any rate.

In the taxi I thought, Well, why not? The situation is quite different now, after all. You only had to say no. But yet, I couldn't quite avoid an obscure feeling of loss. Loss of friendship, or something like it, perhaps? I hadn't wanted intimacy. Not with Yves. Not for a long time with anyone. It may well have been why I had taken refuge in what was probably the over-critical.

Thinking about this as the taxi approached Victoria station I had the idea that if I had been writing about it I would have described my feeling as like going into a shop to make a quite valued regular purchase, only to find that it was now out of stock, and that something different, unwanted, had been offered instead.

My train was unusually full. Sitting next to me was an old lady with dirty, broken nails. I noticed the nails when after a time she began to eat a stale-looking cheese roll which she had had in a paper bag. I found it curiously disturbing, I can't exactly explain why, that she should be old and shabbily dressed and eating a stale cheese roll with battered hands.

Once or twice she smiled at me, a comradely, tongue-clicking "That's life" smile.

When she reached her destination, and for reasons which had more to do with me, I think, than with her — there were half a dozen other people who would have done it — I lifted her case down from the rack.

At Whitethorn I got into my car and drove quickly home.

SEVEN

"Shhh," Joanna said. "He's fast asleep."

She stood in the hall. She had on jeans, and a plain white shirt open at the neck. Briefly, on a complete impulse, I put my arm round her.

"Do you want something to eat?"

"I want something to drink," I said.

She laughed. "Are you out of practice for London?"

"Out of practice. I don't know if for London. Was Hugh all right?"

"He was fine. We looked at the horse book. Twice. Go and sit down, and I'll see what there is to find. Did you know that it's going to snow?" I looked in first at Hugh and replaced his coverlet. He lay, one small arm under his head, breathing softly. I felt a hand. He was quite warm.

What Joanna found was a bottle of whisky untouched for months. It was that or nothing. She moved her geography notes off a little table.

"Can I have some?" she said. "As we're celebrating."

"Of course. But what are we celebrating?"

"That you've come back early." She drank too much of the whisky quickly, and it made her cough. "Hell, Roz, that's strong. Not nasty, though." She drank a little more. "Weren't you having a nice time? It's a long way to go for not having a nice time."

"I suppose so." I smiled at her. "Peter does it every day. Not that he has to clock on and off," I said, realizing as soon as I'd said it that it was quite irrelevant.

"And a lot of fare," Joanna was remarking, practically. It was the kind of observation that in my financially calculating situation, I tried not to make. But when she made it I nodded.

"Was Parliament any good? Did you have a guided tour?"

"No. It was just something a friend of Yves' arranged. We had a quick look round, which was interesting, but it was really just for the debate."

"What was the debate about?"

"Sole, mostly."

"Soul?" Joanna said, sounding surprised. "The what-shall-it-profit-a-man-if-he-gain-the-whole-world-and-lose-it kind of soul?"

"No. Dover sole."

"Oh, *bonne femme* kind of sole."

"*You* would have got on splendidly with Yves."

"Didn't you?" She offered me the plate of crackers she had buttered. Already color was appearing in her usually pale face, as it had done at the Johnny Onion. "I thought you quite liked him. What went wrong? What did he do?"

"Nothing. It was just that he started being different. And after nine years of having a pen-friend I didn't want the trouble of having anything else."

"So you made for the door?"

"I told him I had to come home to you."

But she didn't laugh. It was her turn to nod. Then she said, thinking about it, "Nine years," and added, "you were married at my age."

"A bit more."

There was a pause before she said, looking at me, "You don't like things starting to be different? I do. I wait for it to happen."

"Do you?"

"Couldn't it have been fun to have Yves different? I mean, interesting?"

"No."

"You wouldn't have needed to be in love with him."

"No, I agree."

"There was never the wildest possibility of my ever being in love with Steve."

"Tell me about Steve." I was conscious of the whisky beginning to have its effect.

"Oh, Roz," she said. "He was quite *incredible* to look at. *Marvelous.* I wish you could have seen him. Though I suppose you never will. And he laid siege to me. It isn't easy to lay siege to somebody in a convent."

"I imagine."

"He climbed up things, and put notes under things, and pretended he was a gardener. He even told the

Reverend Mother he'd been sent to mend a leak in the roof — and, Roz, she *believed* him!"

"He must have been persuasive," I said, laughing. "Though to be fair to her I suppose there was no real reason why she shouldn't. When people say they're gardeners or plumbers or whatever they usually are."

"But he had feet of clay," Joanna said.

I waited, and she helped herself to a cracker.

Then I said, "Ever since I heard about it, about you, when you were just someone Cassie and Peter had started to talk about, I've wondered what went wrong."

"Have you?" She made a small grimace. "Well, I can tell you. It won't take long. It started off all right. No, it didn't really. I don't think he was very good at making love — though who am I to say? But as soon as my geography teacher entered left, and everything got into the papers, that was too much for him. He just said it could spell Trouble, with a capital T, and made off back to camp. He even left a note to tell me." She added, self-mocking, "Ditched. Left high and dry. Abandoned — to the Swan."

I wasn't quite sure what to make of the self-mockery, looking at her, and after a moment I said, "What was it like at the Swan?"

"It was all right," she said. "I ached everywhere at first but I was getting used to it. It wasn't as restful as the convent. You know, Roz, the convent *was* quite restful, even with our work. And I feel as if I never, never want to be restful again in all my life." We emptied our glasses. "The people at the Swan were quite nice, really. They said they'd promote me to barmaid on my birthday. Ought we to drink any more?"

"Probably not. But I'm going to. Just a bit."

"So we'll drink to Yves," she said. "For sending you back early."

"All right." We drank to Yves.

There was a silence. Then she said, "Now you tell me about Tom." I realized I had frowned. "I'll let you off the book until it's finished. But how can I know you if you don't talk to me about Tom? I mean —" Her voice became hesitant. "I mean," she said again, "about Tom being killed."

"I know that's what you mean. I don't know if I can, Joanna." Her voice had been hesitant, but her gaze was direct. "It would be the first time. To anyone."

"So. We're friends. Special friends, aren't we?"

"Yes."

"Tell me about Tom."

*****

Something about her insistence, less coercive than a rather gentle statement of her will, somehow opened the way for me that evening to say out loud what I hadn't before said, to put it into words, however poor the words. "It was dreadful. It shouldn't have happened. He had had five years of the war. A bad war for him. He was in Yugoslavia. And then in the Ardennes. And he survived all that. And he was killed by a mishap. A slip."

"Yes?" She spoke gently.

"They were absailing. Coming down. A rock got dislodged. It was senseless. Pointless. It didn't mean anything. All it meant was that he hasn't had his life and Hugh hasn't got a —"

"Yes. Yes. I know," she said. Then she added, "Roz, you can cry if you want to."

"You see, I don't think I want to cry now." I had a sudden feeling of tenderness towards her, the oval-shaped grave face, the generosity of her absorbed attention. "I think I just want to say it over and over again. Say that it was stupid, senseless, it didn't do any good or achieve *anything* whatever way you look at it. I want to say *that.*"

"You can say it to me. Whenever you want to you can say it to me. and I'll agree with you."

"It won't make very riveting conversation."

Then she smiled. It took me by surprise when she asked, "How much were you in love with him? I mean, it was early, lucky to have found someone to be in love with."

I thought. "I don't really know. *In* love. He was nice. Oh, Joanna, he was nice. And attractive. And he came home from Germany in a marrying mood. And I suppose there was something glamorous, oh, I don't know the word, something like that, about marrying him."

"How much older was he?"

"Eleven years."

Joanna paused. "Would it have lasted?"

"Yes. Yes, I think so."

"Are you the type?"

"I suppose I am."

She made no reply to this, and for a moment neither of us said anything.

"I'll say it just once more. It was a *stupid* thing to have happened. But I won't go on about it now." I made an effort. "Joanna, tell me something. Have you got a passport?"

"Yes," she said. "Of course."

"What color does it give for your eyes?"

"Hazel. Why?"

"I just wondered."

Again there was the silence. "The hell," she said suddenly, "it's difficult not to think about Tom." She poured herself about a quarter of an inch of whisky and gave me an inch. "Do you know the most dreadful thing that ever happened to me?" Then as if reading my thoughts she went on, "It wasn't my mother. That made me sad. But I understood about her. I love my mother. And she loves me. And one day it'll all be all right. Will you laugh if I tell you about my dreadful thing?"

"I'm sure I won't."

"I was about thirteen. A friend at school had given me two white mice. I had them in a cage at the bottom of the garden. Then I went to stay with my grandmother, and I'd forgotten about them. I didn't leave them any water or food or anything. And when I came back they'd had babies, little red things, all of them cooped up in this cage. So many. So many. And I didn't know what to do about it. The whole thing had got too much. And my mother didn't know, either. And she made our doctor — she knew him quite well, you see — come and chloroform them. And Roz, do you know, all of that's the only thing in my life that has really made me feel wicked. I have dreams about it. I have dreams about them all cooped up in that cage because I forgot them. Do you have a dream, over and over?"

"I don't want to laugh. Poor mice. Poor Joanna."

It astonished me that I could be about to tell her something that I had never told anybody, ever before. But nevertheless I did it. "I dream that I am being left out of something. It's never the same thing. It could be a party. Or people in another room. But it's always the same idea. Once it was that everyone else was up on a platform, and I wasn't."

"Roz," Joanna said. And she came over to where I was sitting, and bent down to kiss me. Momentarily as she did so I was aware of her breasts, bra-less under the white shirt. "Well you're not being left out of anything now. We're together in your room and it's nice. I didn't know Mrs. Hallam had anything so nice to offer. I like your room. It's a home, you know. In spite of what happened. I want to buy you something for it. So that you'll always remember me. What would you like?"

"Oh, Joanna, I don't know," I said as she returned to the chair opposite me. "But that reminds me. I have something for your birthday."

It was an enlargement of a photograph of Barbary that I had taken for Hugh. I had had the enlargement put in a wooden frame.

"Roz," she said. "Darling."

It was the first time she had called me that. Then she added, "And tomorrow I have to go. But I will be back for Mrs. Hallam's 'Entertainment.' "

In bed later I thought about the "firsts" of the evening.

EIGHT

Mrs. Hallam's 'Entertainment' coincided not with the forecast snow which had still to arrive but with a ferocious drop in temperature. However, this appeared to have no discernible effect on the size of the audience.

The event, which had been running for years and always along the same lines, had turned into something of a traditional social occasion. Held in the main hall of the civic center between about six-thirty and eight-thirty, while a separate entertainment was organized for the young children in a nearby room known as the Birthday

Room, it was in aid of schools' equipment, and served proper coffee.

The first part was devoted largely to the singing of such songs as "The Lass with the Delicate Air" by little boys clearly not at home, as Alison once put it, in the idiom, and the reciting of poems. There were also piano solos which, while they varied in length and degree of difficulty, were performed on the whole with a uniform sturdiness.

The second half, in the hands of a drama teacher who had an attachment bordering on a fixation to the proposition that all children, anyone's as much as her own, should live up culturally to the best that was in them, was always Scenes from Shakespeare.

None of this, though, seemed enough to account for the unfailing success of the evening. Perhaps the only explanation was Mrs. Hallam herself, with her warm, ubiquitous annual presence projecting interest and personal friendliness, successfully making an art form of physical contact, the kiss in welcome, the arm briefly round a shoulder — a difficult thing to do.

Pushing a way through with Hugh to the Birthday Room, I found the thought entering my head that maybe she had advisedly chosen such an improbable, far from universally convenient day as Christmas Eve, in order to avoid an embarrassing overflow. To my satisfaction Hugh joined the other children with no more than a brief glance backwards.

In our row Alison was talking to Peter and his father. One or two of the people staying with Peter and Cassie had come, others had preferred the fire. Cassie was helping. It was all very laissez-faire. A seat had been kept for Joanna in case she should arrive in time.

"*Twelfth Night,*" Alison was saying, "James has seen. So one way and another, and taking everything into account, I did think probably he'd be better at home this year. All that correspondence! And the *misconceptions*! Really, don't you feel yourself, Mr. Turner, once is enough for anybody? — unless, of course, you happen to be an addict. And I'd never say James was a Shakespeare addict. I'd say if anything he wasn't. I'm not too fond of *Twelfth Night* myself. But *I* seem to keep seeing Sylvia Hallam. He only sees her once a month." A child in pigtails appeared on the stage.

It was when the performance of a Beethoven bagatelle was about to begin that I saw Joanna, the collar of her raincoat turned up so that her hair broke on it. She was in murmured conversation at the side of the hall with Mrs. Hallam. After a moment she slipped into her seat. "Nice to be back," she said softly to me. As the performance of the bagatelle was being applauded she added, "My father was very good. I think he's just thankful to have me here. Out of harm's way. But by the end of the time we'd even run out of fish talk."

Fish talk, I thought, before I realized she was referring to the kind of conversation Yves and I had made.

With the interval and the coffee she said, "All right, Roz?"

"Yes," I said, and smiled at her.

Alison was already explaining to friends why it was that *Twelfth Night* had never really been a favorite play of hers.

"Not ever since we saw Roger in the role of what's his name? — Fate, or something."

"Feste," Joanna said, beginning to laugh.

"The very same. Look." She pointed to her program. "He had two expressions, Roger, ennui and boundless astonishment, and played them off against each other like rivals. While Viola, poor girl, kept wringing her hands and looking sorely troubled. We were never altogether clear whether it was part of the plot. Do you really suppose anyone over around Hugh's age ever feels as astonished about *anything* as people seem to be on the stage? In real life, I mean. My own feeling about life is that what happens is what you expected to happen —"

"No," Joanna and I said together, then looked at each other.'

"Only we don't all expect the same thing, do we?" Cassie said.

But before we could go into this other friends of Alison's had come up to her and she began to tell them about Bill Moon. "This year for Christmas," she said, "we have a seafarer. An old man of the sea. I'll say one thing for my son, you never know what to expect next. Once after he had moved on from his signal triumph as Feste we had two thirds of a washboard group. I'm sure that's what they said, though I found it hard to believe at the time. Refined by centuries of aristocratic inbreeding they were not."

"We must all be very glad you've brought him up to be so broad-minded," Peter said.

"Brought him up! It's a defect of character. God knows where he gets it from. It must go back a long way. Ah, I do believe the curtain stirred."

It was scenes from *Twelfth Night.* Walls trembled and doors stuck with the familiarity, almost endearing of a cliché. The drama teacher here and there prompted, her strong voice not merely audible, but suggestive of inhibited passion.

Alison glanced at me. "You can always tell a good scene from Shakespeare," she murmured, "from the way it makes you go hot."

Just as the last scene was ending she disappeared and returned hand in hand with Hugh. "We may not all of us distinguish ourselves in the area of being fruitful and multiplying," she said; and I saw Joanna frown. Though most of my mind was on Hugh, some small part of it somewhere wanted to say it's all right, it doesn't matter, it's only Alison. Alison went on, "But we can rest assured others are making up for us. God, what a bun fight. Roz, dear, Hugh is coming to see my decorations. He's not at all tired. What about you? Are you coming? One must expect the drama to impose a certain amount of strain in any circumstances. So I have assembled a little something to pull us round."

Thus pre-empted, I laughed, and said, "Yes to the decorations; no to the assemblage."

"What assemblage?" Roger seemed to have appeared from nowhere out of the crowd.

"You've missed the best of it," his mother said ironically.

"You think so?" He put an arm round her. "I've just been talking to Mrs. Hallam. She sends her love and says she'll look in for a few minutes when she's sorted things out here. Hallo, Roz. Joanna." He continued to Joanna with a smile, "Not even you work on Christmas Eve. We're having a party. You're coming, aren't you?"

"Oh," she said. "Well, actually, I was going home. I came straight here and I'm so hungry."

"Hungry?" he said. "Then put all your trust in me," and he linked arms with her. She hesitated.

"Come on," he said again.

He was right about the food. The buffet offered Alison's usual dazzling display and there were Christmas bottles of champagne in support.

The downstairs room at The Tower which Alison used for entertaining really was breathtaking, and after so long I hardly know where to begin in describing it.

Alison was to the best of my knowledge the only person in Whitethorn who had a resident maid, and the parquet shone under the cleverly concealed lighting. The sheepskin rugs had been pushed to one side. There were flowers, and holly and mistletoe, but not too much of it. Alison very rarely referred to her work, but here and there on that evening in small classical gilt frames were several of her illustration originals which had to do with Christmas. And the climax, so to speak, of it all was a huge, natural, fairy-lit, parcel-laden Christmas tree.

Hugh stood gazing at it, his dark eyes wide, mesmerized.

"Quite something, Hugh, isn't it?" Joanna said. Other people came up to speak to him but for a time he remained spellbound.

A young man was playing tunes on the grand piano, surrounded by friends of Roger's.

James dispensed welcome and drinks. "And some fruit cup for Hugh," he said. "Just the thing, I think." At length Hugh accepted his drink, smiling with pleasure as much at the big round glass as at the taste.

Roger was urging food on Joanna. "You can't dance the night away on an aching void," he said. "And this is

Bill," he added, as a solid-looking, middle-aged man with a beard walked over to them. "Roz. Joanna. This is Bill back from sailing the seven seas. Known for treading on his partner's toes in every dance hall from the Falklands to the Faroes. Wherever they are."

"Somewhere off Iceland." Joanna looked up from spreading pâté on the last of a roll. "Danish. I think. Hi, Bill."

Bill Moon wasn't fat but he wasn't far off it. He had alert eyes and an expression which, though extraordinarily good-natured, was far from stupid. His clothes, I am sure, could have caused Alison very little satisfaction.

"Oh yes, of course, the geography buff," Roger was saying. "Bill sings sea shanties in nine different languages."

"Never sung one in my life." He had an accent it was difficult to pin down. Half London, but with something of the West Country in it.

"There, you see. Treads on your toes, can't sing sea shanties. Never be the slightest use to you."

"Oh, I don't know," Joanna said.

The young man at the piano began to play some foot-tapping tune at which Roger held out an arm in invitation. "Better stick with me," he said. "I won't tread on your toes. An interim measure only. You can come back to the pâté."

Perhaps it would have been rather difficult for Joanna to refuse. I couldn't tell from her expression whether she wanted to or not. But as they paused to exchange greetings with the group round the piano and I heard her laugh I could see that she was slipping into a party mood as easily as earlier she had slipped unobtrusively into her seat at the entertainment.

I said to Bill, "Have you found your yacht yet?"

"I've found the yacht," he said. "All I've got to do now is find the money."

"Is it nice?"

"It's wonderful. Built in Sweden. She's a lady, anyone can see that. But she's called a Dutchman. A man of iron."

"It seems rather complicated."

"Not really. She's wonderful," he said again, in the voice, it seemed to me, he might have used if talking about a person.

Alison was giving Hugh his present off the tree.

Bill said, "I'm afraid I'm not much of a dancer. Two left feet. But if you'd like —"

"No, I'm not staying." I smiled at him.

Roger and Joanna had resumed their dancing. I said goodbye to Alison and James. "Can I open it?" Hugh said of his present.

"We'll put it with the other things for the morning, shall we? Let's go home now and switch *our* Christmas tree lights on." I went to say goodbye to Joanna.

"You don't have to go yet," she said.

James had taken Hugh to get his coat. "Hugh must go to bed," I said, "if he's not to be impossible tomorrow." And besides, I thought suddenly, surprised by the intensity of my thought, this isn't *our* Christmas, *our* party; if it's yours, all right.

I might have known then that I was in love.

Joanna hadn't replied to my remark about Hugh.

"I won't be long," she said.

No? I thought, as one of Roger's friends came to ask her to dance.

Outside our own house, where already on the still and deeply frosty air we could hear the sounds of Peter and

Cassie's gathering, I said to Hugh, "Shall we see if we can get upstairs without anyone hearing?"

* * * * *

When he was asleep I put his pillow case of presents at the bottom of his bed. Very late I heard Joanna come back, and go to the small spare room where a bed had been made up for her. There was the running, briefly, of water, then silence.

After a long time I got up to go to the bathroom myself. The air in the passage struck like ice. The house, big and old, wasn't easy to heat.

On my way back, Joanna said, "Good night, Roz."

"Good night. Joanna, are you warm enough?"

There was a pause. "I've been warmer."

"I haven't got any more blankets. Cassie's got them all."

"It doesn't matter."

"It seems a bit silly." I hesitated. "Look, my room's warmer. And there are two blankets on my bed. Do you want to come in with me?"

"Yes," she said. "Can I?"

We lay at first a little separate. "It's nice," she said. "Warm."

I don't know what I had intended by the invitation over and above its face value; I still think not anything. But I dare say any self-respecting analyst would laugh at me.

In any case I found a curious novelty in being in bed with her — I hadn't with anyone, since Tom. Except Hugh. And children don't count, quite apart from that they're children. For them it is so unself-conscious, incidental. With her, there was a kind of special pleasure in it, subtle and potent, a potent pleasure, in the murmured sentences and the comfortable dark, in the intimacy.

We are moved by strange impulses in our relations with one another, impulses not axiomatically connected with sex. At times we reject intimacy, resenting it as we resent the man or woman who stands too near us in the Underground, or the friend who over-presumes. But at other times, when all the mysterious necessary conditions have been fulfilled, we want and need it, mutually responding to break down our own isolation.

"Roz," she was saying tentatively, "there's something I want to tell you" — how differently the same words can be said, it occurs to me now, looking back and remembering; almost the same words — "about why I stayed at Alison's."

"Why shouldn't you have stayed? It was going to be a nice party. Perhaps if I —"

"Listen. When I've been at home, after I've been with —" She stopped, and I knew she had been about to say "after I've been with my father;" perhaps it was some sense of family that prevented her from going on. "After I've been at home," she said again, "now that my mother isn't there, it sort of colors me. It almost makes me feel like someone else. Can you understand that? I have to shake it off. Sometimes I can do it quickly. Sometimes it takes a long time, days. I knew tonight I could do it quickly at Alison's. Everything was bright and somehow rather splendid there tonight. You saw? But it wasn't that I didn't want to be with you." She added, "I could have spent Christmas with Pauline, and I was going to, only I didn't because I did want to be with you."

I had the feeling, though really I knew it was ridiculous, that I had been released from some unhappiness. In reply to her words I felt for her hand.

"There's one thing I wish you'd seen," she said. "Alison dancing with Bill Moon. Wrapped in conversation, they were. Simply wrapped."

"I wish I had seen it. But Alison isn't predictable. The inside of Alison isn't the same as the outside. I've learned that." Her hair touched my face.

"Talk to me," she said.

"What are your favorite things?"

"Cobnuts and pinks."

"And lilac? And wall flowers? I think wall flowers have the most erotic smell I know."

"Do you? I think 'L'apres-midi d'un Faun' has the most erotic sound I know."

"Do you?"

We laughed, but from something other now, I think, than amusement. Perhaps tension.

"You could put it in a book. The wall flowers, I mean. How is your book?"

"Two more chapters."

"Will you write about *falling* in love? One day."

"Perhaps."

"We're meant to enjoy things," she said. "We're meant to be happy. My mother understood that. The nuns didn't. I'm sure they believed at heart if it was nasty it was good for you and if it was nice it wasn't."

"The hair shirt."

"If you mustn't thwart God's will by making life easier, why can you by making it worse?"

"I don't know."

"We didn't take much notice. I think sometimes we felt we just had to be rather kind and tactful because of what they weren't going to have."

There was a silence.

"Do you know," she said, "Steve couldn't believe that it made me feel good to have my back stroked. He said it was just fancy. Wasn't that extraordinary?"

"Wasn't it unimaginative?"

She moved, and a draught passed through the bed. I was conscious now of the heat she was generating at my side.

"You didn't ask me my *unfavorite* things," she said.

"What are your unfavorite things?"

"Mustard. And marmalade. And I don't like tea, much.

"My friend Pauline told me she heard some actress or other say once God had created sex as a joke and when nobody laughed He decided to make it a sin. You know, Pauline really got on with Steve better than I did. He just happened to want me. But she was nice about it. Women aren't like men put them in books, are they? Some men." She seemed to consider this. "Oh, well, anyway, it's great about the wall flowers."

Once more she changed her position. Two coat hangers fell off the bed. "Subsidence," she said, but she didn't laugh.

She was lying now propped on her elbows, gazing down at me. It was light enough to see an indistinct impression of her face, serious, intent.

Then her face came down to mine, her mouth found my mouth, and she kissed me. There was no mistaking the nature of the kiss. Or of my response; it was like a warm thrust at the heart of my sexuality.

"Is it all right?" she said then, and even as she said the words I was aware of their to me touching absurdity. "It's how I feel."

"It's all right."

"I didn't know it could feel like this."

"I didn't know." I drew her against me. And for what seemed a long time we lay tense, and still, except for our trembling — until she undid her jacket, and I buried my face, that was burning, into the flesh between her breasts.

As I began to touch her over the thin pajamas — tentatively, unsure, for it was new to me — her back, her waist, that led softly to thighs, the inside of her legs, she said, "I love you."

Lying against her I could feel through the thin cotton with a kind of disbelief, and a growing joy, the dampness of her excitement. It was then that we sought each other's nakedness, and the love making that went with it.

The climax for both of us that first occasion was quick, overwhelming, seeming to spill from us like some sort of beautiful, unsolicited gift.

Afterwards we were silent, shaken by the force of it, for which we had been unprepared, the joy — its easy, natural force.

It seems to me strange, now, that never once did we feel any need to discuss the nature of our love, to explain, name it, put it into some category. It didn't seem strange at the time. We had begun to love each other. Just that.

Touching her face at length I found the small scar. "How did that happen?"

"Forceps. I didn't want to be born. But, oh, I'm glad I was." Then bending over to kiss me again, she said, "Happy Christmas. Darling. Darling."

NINE

Christmas that year has for me now an almost kaleidoscopic quality with at its center the glow of a newly discovered sensuality, loving, developing — each picture touched with a special joy. Hugh in his peach dressing gown opening his Christmas presents, surrounded by colored paper, while Joanna sat at the end of his bed. Joanna riding Barbary — the first snow on her hair — to the delight of a Hugh she had let put on her riding hat. Snowballing with Roger and Bill Moon.

And there was the organization of the love affair itself. I could I suppose have simply told Cassie that Joanna was sharing my room because it was so cold and this would have caused little or no comment. But somehow to take advantage of this seemed almost like a denial of the relationship, a fundamental dishonesty quite different in kind from saying, as I did, that the wind was catching the door at the top of my stairs and that I was going to lock it. For the first time since being in the house.

Then there was Hugh.

"Does he come into your room at night?" Joanna asked.

"Never. Only in the mornings. If he wants me he calls. But it could change."

"Suppose he came and found us making love, he would only find something beautiful."

"I know. I know that. Darling, I agree with you. But I'd want it to be when he can understand, and not by accident." That I said "when" perhaps gave away how much I was already seeing her in my future.

She nodded at what I had said. And eventually each night when he was asleep we lodged a tin of bricks against the inside of his slightly open door and always had our dressing gowns near at hand.

Hugh and I had our own Christmas dinner.

On Boxing Day, after the supper that Joanna and I helped Cassie get ready, we joined in the party downstairs. Some of us sat 'round the fire, the room pleasantly lit by Peter's yacht reading lamp, and amused ourselves with the page of quizzes, intelligence tests and the like that one of the Sunday "heavies" had devised to help its readers through Christmas.

Even this was lovely for each time Joanna's eyes met mine, the message was, soon we will take off our clothes and be in each other's arms.

There was a problem, I remember, about marbles in a bag — some of them were red, and some of them were green, and you were supposed to know from the information given how many of them were red. Joanna thought about it, and then announced that it had to be done with algebra. Confident in my inability to do anything with algebra I left her to it.

In due course she said she'd come to the conclusion that there were a hundred and thirty-seven red marbles in the bag, which didn't seem likely since red and green together totalled only a hundred.

Peter took her piece of paper. "What do you mean by $19x = 20y - 7$?" he asked.

"I don't know. Is that what I've written? It's only the beginning, isn't it?"

"Oh. Yes. It goes from strength to strength," Peter said.

She laughed. "Let's do the Personality Test," she said.

We gathered from this that she was one of "life's adventurers" and that, if my answers were anything to go by, I wasn't.

Much later that night she came quietly to my room. "Here I am," she said.

"I wondered who it might be."

She smiled and said, "Roz, now I'm eighteen I've got some money through my grandmother. I don't mean an heiress or anything like that. But enough. More than I need. Can we just forget about electricity bills? Make the room so hot that we can hardly breathe? Would that be all right?"

"That would be all right," I said.

And sitting in front of the fire naked after we had made love and drinking hot milk, because this was what she had said she wanted, I learned a new enchantment, the enchantment of looking. The dusty pink encircling the nipples of her small breasts. Her legs tucked under her. The light from the fire shining on her spine which ended with the cleft I had only to see to want to touch, and then to touch all of her. A well of sensual feeling had been tapped that was to stay with me for always.

I caressed her as we talked. "Did I tell you that I love you?"

"I believe you did mention something of the sort." But she couldn't keep it up and she came to my arms and we held each other and said the sort of things lovers do say.

A little later she asked, "Do you think it is easier to fall in love with women?"

"I suppose it depends who you are. And what 'women.' "

"Could you fall in love with Roger?"

"No."

"Did you go to a mixed school?"

"Yes."

"Did you like it?"

"Yes."

"Is that where you met Tom?" she said.

"No. He'd left, anyway. I met him at church."

"At church?" she said, sounding surprised. "I didn't think you were religious."

"I wasn't, really. I went with friends. I'm not. I'm a Don't Know-er."

"Did your parents like Tom?"

"They loved him."

"Perhaps that helped. I mean —" She paused. She had meant, the accident.

"It didn't, really. I've never been able to talk to my parents about Tom. Couldn't to anyone. I can't. Only to you." I looked at her.

And again desire for her began to stir in me like a joy in those early days that, taking me by surprise, could never be satisfied.

"It *is* beautiful, isn't it?" she said. "We don't want to hurt each other. Nobody else would do. We just want to love." Then she said, "Do you love your parents?"

"I love both of them," I said. "But I don't feel close to either of them."

"I wish you hadn't got to go."

"We have two more nights."

On the last night before Hugh and I went to stay with my parents we lay wishing it wasn't nearly morning.

"Peter thanked me for letting them have my room," Joanna said. "*Thanked* me! He said he supposed I'd be glad to get it back. Roz, last night I dreamed about the mice. How could that be? Now? With you?"

"Perhaps where we dream doesn't know about now, with me." I held her very close and found a trace of tears on her face.

"I don't want you to go," she said again.

"It's not for long."

"It won't be so easy when you get back."

"But it will be all right."

*****

Although it was three hundred and something to one against, Hugh and I shared a birthday at the beginning of January. It was neither here nor there. It had no particular effect on our lives, except that it tended to make for concentrated celebrating.

In the afternoon my mother, already happy because she had found her sister better than she expected, and in her element anyway with young children, gave him a birthday party.

It was an occasion of much noise and much merriment; much cheerful squandering of time. For time, to children, must appear an unrationed commodity, like water from a tap. At six or seven they are still infinitely far from the moment when they will realize all at once that there is a limit on what is left and that the most must be made of it.

Cushions were hurled, and blobs of jelly trodden into the carpet. Traditional party games were played, and as the afternoon wore on, much more exciting ones invented. The truculent little boy who wanted bombs — we discovered from an indignant Hugh that what he had said was that there would be bon-bons — was to some extent pacified with more crackers, and more pricked balloons. Eating was resumed at irregular intervals.

Hugh said that the man who did the conjuring tricks was better than Mrs. Carnaby's friend's son, who had done them for the children at Mrs. Hallam's 'Entertainment:' which was as well, for he could just as easily have said that he wasn't.

And then it was all over.

I was glad that before all the clearing up began I was to walk home with a small, delicate-looking girl in a white blouse whose parents were recovering from 'flu. (I made a mental note not to go into the house. The last thing I wanted was 'flu.)

As I came back along the Swanage front I knew it was because of Joanna that the smell of the winter sea, the line of the hills just visible in the fading light, the texture of the Purbeck stone itself were all heightened, intensified for me and somehow marvelous as never before though so familiar.

Back at my parents' home Hugh was talking to my mother about the cog and chain system on the Poole Harbour ferry that had intrigued him on the way down. The Dorset names he spoke of, Sandbanks, Shell Bay, had for me a touch of magic.

In the evening my father took us all out to dinner to that miracle in an English town, somewhere attractive to eat well and dance. It was called the XYZ Club, and my father was a member largely because it was much used by a local group interested in anthropology. Anthropology was my father's passion. Tom and I had had bets about how long it would be before the subject came up.

However, first we had a story for Hugh, after the wine had been ordered, about Clos de Vougeot.

"When you are seventy-four, young man," my father said, "you will see what the French soldier means."

He tipped his glass, and, true to my mood, the shafts of light in the deep red wine danced, I thought, like lithe, leaping figures in a ballet.

It is too much, I told myself. I am stupidly happy. But it was without in the least minding.

"What soldier?" Hugh said.

"When a French regiment passes this particular vineyard," my father told him, pointing to the label, "it presents arms."

"It's a kind of salute," my mother explained.

Hugh thought for a moment, then said, "When I pass his field, I'm going to salute Barbary."

In honor of my birthday, my father invited me to dance. I was conscious of people smiling at me, and knew with affection that he must appear something of a fairy tale father — white-haired, pink-cheeked, plump. "You look well, Roz," he said. "The writing's going all right, is it?"

I smiled. My first novel had not been the kind of book that either of my parents had enjoyed very much, but they had been pleased, and polite. They would like to have been proud of the next one.

"I'm glad you're giving it a rest now though," he said. "Doesn't do to keep at it too much. Bad for your eyes."

I wasn't in any real sense "giving it a rest." I had been completely unable since Christmas Eve to concentrate and had been astonished that Joanna could work without difficulty.

It must have been two or three weeks before this phase passed for me.

Back at the table, and fresh from some conference or other, my father began to discourse firmly on the probable birthplace of "*Man.*" He referred to the Hologenists, who believe — I knew before I knew how to boil an egg — that "*Man*" appeared simultaneously in a number of different places, and then he proceeded to disagree with them.

"So you see," he said, "the evidence piling up clearly indicates that we evolved from whatever we were into Man in some quite limited area. Man is a naked animal. It's highly probable he could only have originated under tropical or sub-tropical conditions."

Hugh yawned and his gaze turned toward the sweet trolley. "I want the cake," he said.

"And since Man has a common ancestry with the apes," my father continued, "that means, Hugh, they both came from the same kind of creature, it seems only logical to look for his beginnings where the apes were."

Hugh chose his gâteau maison.

"Where were they?" my mother asked. She was used to her role in this sort of conversation.

"Roughly from Spain to China, and from Egypt to the Transvaal —"

"I want to go to Spain," Hugh said.

That night in bed I longed for Joanna, and dreamed of my return.

* * * * *

She met us both with shining eyes.

TEN

All that, though, was in the 'fifties. Whitethorn in the 'fifties was a different world. Looking back on it over the intervening decades of my life, I have a feeling not of pride exactly but of something resembling it, a feeling of being glad perhaps, that even at that time Joanna and I had no smallest sense of wrongness in the relationship, and would have no particular wish to conceal it had the circumstances been so much as marginally otherwise; but we had no wish either to repay Cassie and Mrs. Hallam with the embarrassment which would have been inevitable were our relationship to become known.

So, the Christmas arrangements at an end, there was for us the immediate problem of how to be safely alone together — not, I suppose, a new one in the long history of love — without drawing attention to why we wanted to be.

We saw each other again with a mixture of joy and frustration.

The next morning, the day before the schools were due to reopen, Joanna went to a prefects' meeting which was for discussing matters related to the smooth running of the school in the coming term: there being a strong tradition of senior pupil participation. She had had no enthusiasm for going but since she had been invited out of pure friendliness and goodwill had felt to refuse would be mannerless.

I heard the front door close, saw her leave the house. Then as if from nowhere Roger appeared offering her a lift, which she accepted. Since Christmas Eve his show of interest had been increased.

I felt restless and undecided. After a while I went down to Cassie to remind her that as it was the New Year we had to put up Mrs. Carnaby's money. However, it was the first thing that she said to me. But she didn't stay to talk. She was on her way out to see Barbary's owners about something or other, I can't remember what — probably how the little girl was getting on at school.

"What can I do?" Hugh said.

"Shall we go and interrupt Alison?"

"Yes," he said, brightening. He loved The Tower and I think he loved Alison.

A certain daring was implicit in interrupting Alison when she was at work. But I knew that he would act as a human breastplate.

He climbed the interminable stairs to her studio completely confident of his welcome, which proved to be quite justified.

She was working on the eyes of a baby leopard and continued with this for a moment or two. Then she said, "There." And she smiled at him. "Surprises can be tricky things. But this is a nice one. Did you know that leopards are born blind?"

"How long for?" he asked.

"About a week. Bit more. Bit less. They have a blue film over their eyes when they're born. A beautiful blue. Well, Roz — do I detect in you the look of someone at a loose end?"

"I couldn't have put it better."

"And you the writer. You disappoint me. Perhaps you're in need of sustenance. I have a provisional arrangement to meet Sylvia Hallam for coffee. I saw her yesterday because she wants James for one of her committees. Very provisional. Which means she may turn up or she may not. However, we could go and find out if the Columbine has any Battenburg on offer."

At this Hugh told her about his gâteau maison, something that seemingly had made quite an impression, though he didn't turn down the idea of the Battenburg.

"You will have to live on lettuce leaves for a month," she told him, "to regulate the disgusting fatty acids in your system," and he laughed.

There was Battenburg on offer. We had just finished our first cup of coffee when he said, "There's Mrs. Hallam" — and there she was, sandalled, casually dressed as always, looking busy.

"I can't stay more than ten minutes," she said. "Less. I'm already late for Colonel Tobin."

"Magistrates should be made to wait," Alison said. "It keeps them in touch with the real world."

"But the real world for me," Mrs. Hallam said and smiled, "is that he runs our sports fund. Roz, it's nice to see you looking so well. How was Swanage?"

"Wonderful."

"Remarkable what a breath of sea air will do."

"You know," Alison said, "I'm being driven to the conclusion that pure passion is a force to be reckoned with, no matter where, for God's sake, it comes from." I looked at her and felt myself color. But she went on, "I am not at all sure that Mr. Moon won't end up having me take a run over to look at this legendary yacht of his. Not that that isn't a far cry from lending him any money."

"Were you thinking of lending him money?" asked Mrs. Hallam, who seemed to know about Bill Moon.

"Thinking is too strong a word."

"He's very enamored," I said.

"According to him it's a pleasing sight. But safe with it. Anyway, the drive's pleasant enough. Now the weather's milder, thank God. Would all or any of you care to come?"

Mrs. Hallam made a regretful gesture, implying that if only she had the time.

"Me," Hugh said.

"I will enter you in my diary. Underlined. Perhaps you will persuade your mother to come with you."

We talked about the yacht a little longer, and then Mrs. Hallam said, "You will tell me, Roz, won't you, when I can enter you in *my* diary for your book talk? I like to have every month accounted for. Besides, it will be so interesting for the girls. Particularly as you are local."

"Is Roz going to do a book talk?" Alison said. "What a lovely idea. Though I have to warn you, Sylvia, that so far

I have failed to extract from her any inkling of what her new one is about."

It occurred to me suddenly that when literary reticence is becoming a byword it has probably gone too far. "It is about," I said, doing what I could, "a woman who believes that so long as women continue to see as a virtue letting their hearts rule their heads, whatever else happens they will never have equality."

"That is an interesting point of view." Mrs. Hallam finished her coffee. "And I would dearly love to discuss it with you. Roz, I truly would. Another time. But now I have to go."

She had already stood up when she added, "By the way, I'm going to have a word with Cassie about Joanna. And with Joanna herself, of course. She's very bright and she's extremely well organized. We feel at school her best plan now would be to work largely on her own with some supervision for each subject, say once or twice a week. The courses have never quite coincided and we do feel in the circumstances that this would be best."

Before she left she lightly touched my cheek. From most people it might have been an irritation. With her, it was part of her warmth and charm. "Alison," she said, "I'll be in touch."

She waved to Hugh from the street, without the least idea, I am sure, of the gift she had just bestowed on Joanna and me.

"I'm not certain we know all there is to know about her," Alison was saying, "but I have to confess Joanna has not turned out quite as I had envisaged."

*****

What we had been given was the house to ourselves for long periods of time as a part of our ordinary lives. We examined the offering with delight, laid it out, made it into a program. And I have to say really it worked very well. Within, so to speak, the jurisdiction of our program my book was sent off, I began planning the next one, and Joanna — I smile wryly to recall it — got her two As and a B.

Of course there were hiccoughs, to put it like that. I clearly remember one afternoon in particular. Joanna had been to school that morning, and we had arranged that we would work in the afternoon until I had to go and collect Hugh.

We sat at each end of my table. I had just switched on Radion Three. It so happened that we both liked working with background music. They had just begun to play "Scheherazade."

Not many minutes passed before Joanna said, "You know about wall flowers."

"Yes."

"Boxwood is pretty marvelous, too."

"I haven't noticed." I looked up.

"There's some down by the stream. I'll show you." She paused. "I'm not sure this music is helping me concentrate."

"Do you want me to turn it off?"

She made a small expression with her mouth. "We did it once in a music appreciation class. 'Scheherazade,' I mean. It went on rather a long time and Pauline and I wrote a poem about it. A verse each."

I smiled at her and put down my pen. "Do you remember your verse?"

"Of course. One doesn't forget one's masterpieces. It went:

It can't be amusing
to sleep with a cross kind
who has certainly led you
to believe he'll behead you
when day breaks.

The real beauty of it," she added, "resides in the fact that 'breaks' doesn't rhyme with anything." Her face was grave.

"I do appreciate that. Do you remember Pauline's verse?"

"Of course. It would be very egocentric only to remember one's own masterpieces. The great beauty of her verse resides in the fact that you have to hyphenate kidding and have the -ing on a line by itself."

"I'm sure I'll appreciate that, too. How does it go?"

"It goes:

I know I would rather
stay very much farther
from him than she did.
No kidd-
ing."

"I think that is wonderful, of course. But I think yours is better."

She laughed. "I hoped you would. You know, 'Scheherazade' didn't seem to have the same effect on me in the music appreciation class."

"No?"

Quite suddenly then, the changing mood between us took over. Instinctively rather than by design, hardly aware of why I did it, I got up and moved away from the window.

"I like your sweater. It's almost the same color as The Tower's wall. If it had been me I'd have kept their rooms round. I like the color." She had come over to where I was standing.

From behind, she put her hands under the sweater and released my bra, covering my breasts with her hands.

Briefly it passed through my mind that what Yves had done, so little, had created in me merely the wish to resist. Now, what she did, was welcome, causing at once the beginning of excitement, the desire as Frank Sinatra once put it in a song, some song, "Witchcraft" perhaps, but I'm not sure — the desire for her to proceed with what she was leading me to. Her hands lowered, she unzipped my jeans; the hands persuasive, unhurried, knowing in detail their way about — empathetic, exciting.

She said, her face against my back, "Come and love me. Where we did the first time."

In my bed we loved each other, slowly, slowly, used to it now.

When it was over, at last she said, "I love you. You know that. I love you so much. I'm so happy."

"It makes two of us, Joey. It really does."

They were coming to the last of the Russian notes. We lay listening.

"But we must get up," I said. "I have a son to collect."

"I know," she said.

* * * * *

That afternoon, I remember, was after Alison had organized her trip to Stainton.

* * * * *

There were six of us for the trip, one Saturday. James had declined, Cassie had said she was too busy, but Peter had been interested to see the yacht; Roger had invited Joanna. It was all quite preliminary and "off the record" as far as Alison was concerned, she explained to us. She hadn't even mentioned her intention to Bill Moon.

When we started off the weather was quite promising, warmish after another very cold spell, but by the time we reached Stainton it was already raining.

I first saw *The Gold Digger* in a sad, persistent rain. We sat in the car looking at her. She had a long, heavily carved bowsprit, and lee-boards which had just been painted red. One could imagine very big sails, and a great compliment of rigging.

"Isn't she beautiful," Joanna said.

Alison turned to Peter. "What do you think of her?" she said.

"She's certainly beautiful," he said. "And she looks very solid. A splendid touch of the barge about her."

"She's bigger than I thought. Nice and big. Plenty of room," Alison said. "You don't think she looks at all likely to sink?"

"I shouldn't think for a moment she'd do anything so ill-advised."

Or flighty, it occurred to me. She was a seductress, all right, but a seasoned one.

"She's beautiful," Joanna said again.

Roger and Peter got out for a closer look and Joanna followed them, taking Hugh with her. But the rain soon drove them back. We retreated to the "hut," which was separated from the front by a grass-flanked drive, where Roger made tea, which Joanna refused.

After about half an hour the rain eased off and Roger and Joanna said they would take Hugh for a walk.

"Are you coming?" Joanna said to me.

I shook my head. Although the term "hut" gave no real indication of the wooden building's size, it had proved small for confining a six-year-old little boy with nothing much to interest him except other people's possessions seemingly made for breaking or finger marking. Alison didn't appear to mind. But there can't be many parents not thankful from time to time to be relieved of the presence of their children.

"Well, I suppose it'll be good for their lungs," Alison remarked, watching them go. "Anyhow, they'd better make the most of it. Another ten minutes and it'll be pelting down again." She lit a cigarette.

"So you really don't think," she said at length to Peter, "that boat looks a lot of old junk?"

"I certainly don't think it looks that. I'd say she's in very good nick."

"I know Bill Moon's been impressed, to say the least. Not that I'd have anything to do with it without some sort of survey. I suppose you can have boat surveys the way you have house surveys. I don't really believe anything anyone says." She exhaled smoke, thinking about this. "Do you know, only yesterday I heard Roger remark that traditional Christian morality is moribund. Would *you* say it is?"

"Me?" Peter said. "Well I suppose I'd check first on the meaning of moribund."

"I had more trouble with the meaning of traditional Christian morality. Still, taking the two together," Alison said, "I suppose it means that from now on we all start doing exactly what we like. A prospect I view with mixed feelings for other people. Roz, where did Joanna get that anorak? It suits her."

"Her mother sent it."

"Is she interested in clothes? Joanna."

"Quite, I think. I haven't exactly seen her poring over *Vogue.*"

"Would you recognize it?"

I laughed. "That, Alison, is uncalled for. Even on a wet day out." She displayed her hands in mock apology. "And yes, I would. I have a dentist. And a hairdresser."

"Your hair looks very nice," Peter said, kindly. He had not understood, I think, as Joanna had once not understood, as Joanna had learned, that much of what Alison said was no real part of her, was never really designed to upset or put down, but was almost like a script. "Very nice," he said again. I had some sympathy with him. "Nice" is an awkward word to get stuck on. "Natural," he added, finally hitting on something.

Alison was saying, "If I were to depend on the hoary *Vogues* at my hairdresser's, at any rate it would ensure me a hemline starkly at odds with the rest of civilization. There, it's started to rain again. I said it would."

And it was true that drops of rain were once more pitting the broad half-circle of sand we could see from our window. She lit another cigarette.

"I think I'm going to sell this place and get somewhere a bit brighter. Sormes-les-Mimosas, that's what I've got in mind. I don't know where it is, but I've heard of it, and it sounds all right. Don't you think it sounds all right? Peter?" He nodded. "You're seeing a lot of the sea at the moment, Roz. You must be getting quite an expert on ozone. I don't even know whether it is at the sea. But I think it's just what I'm after. Brown and yellow, with a dash of exclusive Gallic style thrown in. Of course, for all I know it might be up to the eyes in tourists. It was James, incidentally, who so took to it *here*. For the fishing." She paused. "Just look at that rain. What are they doing now?"

Roger and Joanna had been sitting on the harbor wall, with Hugh between them. But now, as the rain began to fall faster, they jumped down and ran — running past the one or two wet empty iron seats and on towards the stonework steps. Roger ran with his head lowered, his arms round Joanna and Hugh, one on either side. Her hair was blown about and wet.

"Long, idle summer days we spent swimming, and drying off again in the sun," Alison greeted them. "And the sand was hot where we lay, and the air was a-shimmer; butterflies there were, so help me, and flowers warm from the hedgerows, and if you imagine there was anything slippery and slimy about those chalk paths going down to the sea, I can only say, it's because we've all been cooped up too long in this scepter'd isle."

"The rain in Stainton stays plainly in the main," Roger said.

Joanna glanced at him and laughed, which Alison noted. So, I suppose, did I.

"Which is a very good reason for us all going home," Alison said decisively. "I trust I shall be able to salvage something from this washout. Peter dear, thank you for coming. Roger, you drive. I want to think."

And certainly she was uncharacteristically silent on the way home.

The sky was already a muted mauve, most of its pink was lost with the premature onset of evening. Secretly I took Joanna's hand.

"I'm glad it looked nice and safe," Alison said.

* * * * *

I don't think it came as much of a surprise to any of us when Alison made up her mind eventually to help Bill Moon get his yacht. I was surprised by her terms, but that might only have meant I was slow-witted. Anyhow, we had to wait quite a little while to hear about the terms.

Returning one lunch time from Whitethorn, where I had been to the library and the bank (and, incidentally, noted that the little cinema near the children's playground was going to show a Greta Garbo film), I came upon Joanna and Cassie talking about *The Gold Digger*. They were standing by the stream just outside the wooden gate at the bottom of our garden. The stream was flowing full and fast because of all the rain we had had. Joanna was looking down at it.

Cassie was saying, "Well, now he's got it I don't know what he's going to do with it. I'm sure Alison must have said, but —"

Joanna laughed. "I'm sure she must have done. Alison must have said just about everything there is to say. Roger said for the holiday trade."

"Hallo, Roz. A sail round the bay?"

I said, "I'd have thought a sail round the world would be more in Bill Moon's line." Joanna turned; she engaged my look with hers, and half smiled, without speaking. I suppressed the wish, then, that Cassie wasn't there and that we could be as we were when we were alone together. To include her, to make amends, though she wouldn't have known what for, I said, "I like that brooch. Cassie, *where* did you say you were going tonight?"

"The Kleins. We're having drinks. Yes, Peter bought it in Corsica. By the way, Joanna, that reminds me. They'll ask about Erica and Barbary."

"He knows she's afraid of him."

"How does Roger get on with Barbary?" I asked.

"Roger's quite a good rider. But he's not interested enough. Barbary needs to be more than just ridden."

"They'll simply have to get rid of him, I suppose, in the end?" Cassie said.

"They say they won't until the summer, anyhow."

"That feels a long way away," Cassie said. "Come on, let's go indoors."

Indoors there was a letter for Joanna.

ELEVEN

I imagine there wouldn't be a lot of evidence to support the proposition that being passionately in love necessarily brings out the best in us.

When it came to the events that Joanna's letter foreshadowed I'd like to think at least I behaved out of character, but I'm not sure there is such a thing; I mean, as behaving out of character.

Really, I suppose, it began like this. A week before the Garbo film was due to be shown I asked her if she'd like to come with me to see it. " 'Ninotchka.' On the Wednesday, darling. One of the little boys at school has asked Hugh to tea. I'd have till about six."

To my surprise she hesitated. "What time?" she said.

"The program starts at two."

She continued to hesitate. "I'm not sure I could make it. I might be tied up." I waited for her to go on, but she didn't. Then seeing that I had waited, she said, "Tests on Tuesday and Wednesday."

I looked at her. For the first time I wasn't sure I believed what she had said. It was an unhappy feeling.

As if to deflect the conversation from herself she added, "I once heard my mother say you could tell a person's character from whether they liked Garbo or Dietrich. My mother was Dietrich."

"Well, I'm Garbo."

"I knew you would be." And she came over and kissed me.

I told myself then to let it go, that I didn't want to be the kind of lover who demanded a twenty-four-hour run-down of the other person's life. And it's true that quite quickly I did more or less forget the incident, forgot about the film, not particularly wanting to go without her.

But then the Tuesday of the following week Mrs. Carnaby arrived as usual. Tuesday for the most part was her day. When she came upstairs Joanna was looking at something on a piece of paper torn from her green note pad.

"Well, dear, and how are you?" she asked her. She had decided to like Joanna — characteristically working on the basis that girls generally were more sinned against than sinning — though I think she had felt a little cheated that the newspaper story hadn't resulted from her point of view in more drama.

"I'm very well, thank you," Joanna said. "How are you, Mrs. Carnaby?"

"I'm sure I'd be much better if I were your age." Mrs. Carnaby glanced round for any debris to take into the kitchen, and picked up an empty tissue box. Then she said, "Is Mrs. Turner's phone out of order?" To what extent her next words were ingenuous or to what extent they weren't it was impossible to tell, but she went on, "We just wondered. My dad thought it was you he saw in the call box outside the Crown." She stood looking at Joanna, her expression difficult to interpret.

"I don't think there's anything wrong with the phone," Joanna answered politely and quite coolly. But at Mrs. Carnaby's words, as if it had been a total reflex action, she crushed the piece of paper she was holding to a ball and aimed it at the wastepaper basket. It missed. She saw me notice; she seemed to have second thoughts and made as if to retrieve it when Mrs. Carnaby picked it up and dropped it into the basket, taking them both off into the kitchen, where, as was her custom, she would empty the wastepaper basket into my large, "for upstairs" sanibin.

"We only wondered," she said again as she went.

"Was it you?" I asked her.

"Yes," she said. "I was phoning Pauline." She glanced at her watch. "Roz, I must go."

From the door she gave me a little wave. I returned her wave, but I felt thrown, bewildered even by the suddenness of the way in which the essence of our relationship seemed somehow to have changed.

When Mrs. Carnaby had gone I went into the kitchen and looked at the sanibin. Sometimes if it was full Mrs. Carnaby took it down and emptied it in the dustbin, leaving it for me to bring up later. On this occasion, however, it was only half full and she hadn't done that.

I truly don't think I could have scrabbled. But there was no need. The ball of green paper was there quite visible. I had only to lift it out.

After quite a long time I did. I smoothed it. It read in her handwriting: "Wed. 1:30. Barley Mow. Saloon."

The only Barley Mow I knew was in the back streets of Meering. I had been there once with Tom. It was known for its real ale, but I hadn't liked the place. I read what was written on the piece of paper several times, then I tore it up.

I'm not sure how I felt. Mostly threatened, I think, as if something out of sight might in some obscure way be threatening all that I had so newly discovered, all that for me had been beautiful and releasing and utterly serious.

There was also the desire to know what, as the old, old phrase has it, was going on. And I was no longer quite certain that if I asked Joanna directly I would ever know. I hated my doubts.

I collected Hugh and gave him his tea. After that he resumed a jig-saw puzzle he had started the previous evening. He sat, a small, concentrated figure at the kitchen table, systematically trying to fit one wooden piece into another.

I did my best to turn my mind to what he was doing.

"It's going to be an otter," he explained at my inquiry, without looking up. "And some water, and some grass."

"I suppose all the green bits are grass."

"They might not be. They might be slimy water."

"And the blue ones painted grass?"

He laughed but when I, too, began experimenting with the curly, to me hostile pieces — I have never been able to do jig-saws — he said, "It's all right, Mummy, *I* can do it."

I put my arm round him a moment, and touched his face with mine before going into the other room. He moved his head slightly away, impatient of the interruption. But, "Your hair's soft," he said to me, still intent on his puzzle.

I took from my bookshelf the copy of the Shakespeare *Sonnets* that Joanna had given me. I had already had a copy, but no book in my possession was more treasured than this one, that she had given me. On the flyleaf she had written, small, simply "J for R." Next to it she had circled "LXXV."

When I turned to this sonnet I read:

So are you to my thoughts as food to life,
Or as sweet season'd showers are to the ground;
And for the peace of you I hold such strife,
As 'twixt a miser and his wealth is found;
Now proud as an enjoyer, and anon'
Doubting the filching age will steal his treasure;
Now counting best to be with you alone,
Then better'd that the world may see my pleasure;
Sometime all full with feasting on your sight,
And by and by clean starved for a look;
Possessing or pursuing no delight
Save what is had or must from you be took.
    Thus do I pine and surfeit day by day,
    Or gluttoning on all, or all away.

Under it she had penciled, "Well, sort of, darling Roz."

I could hear her laughter.

Next I began to tidy my desk. I sorted out such useless items as old Paris bus tickets, and blunted pieces of pencil, placing them in various compartments as though they were objects of value, throwing nothing away, scarcely thinking what I was doing. Then closing the lid of the desk with sudden near decision I thought, "What *is* all this, anyway?"

But I believe it was really because for the rest of that day and the next morning Joanna rather skillfully avoided me that I did what I did.

*****

I couldn't face the public bar alone. Anyhow, I didn't know what it was that I intended to do — whether to try to remain unnoticed, whether to speak to her, or whether only that if I had to. It was like starting a chapter without a plan. That can be done, of course.

The Barley Mow was somber and cheerless, uncentral to say the least. I had been misdirected down the wrong side street, and one fifteen had struck before I succeeded in discovering where the pub was.

Not one of the faces that glanced up, automatically, mildly interested, as I entered the saloon bar was known to me, or meant anything at all. I felt a sense of reprieve. Having pushed open the door, unwillingly, at the spur of my decision, and looked in, not knowing what to expect, I was thankful to find nothing. I had to take no action, endure no reaction.

The saloon had dark-painted irregular walls, and green tiles, and it smelled slightly of stale beer. Already one or two ocher-flecked pools lay on some of the round-topped tables. Among the line of men at the bar, most of them probably farmers, two were arguing.

I carried my drink to a single small table in a corner more or less obscured by the huge jutting fireplace. I was conscious of the occasional glance appraising me. Every time the street door opened I felt a sense of heightened tension. With the passing of the minutes I began to experience something approaching panic. The insides of my hands became damp, leaving moist traces on everything I touched, my handbag, the table top, the curve of my glass. I thought, this is an intolerable thing, I have no right to do it, just to sit here, to wait, to spy.

I looked around me. There was something almost frightening in the place itself, in the dark ugliness of it, and the unfamiliarity of the people, their strangeness. What can any of it possibly have to do with either of us? I thought.

I drank my whiskey, tried to dismantle the appalled and shrinking part of my mind. I stared at things, stared at the people. The large woman in black, with the imposing face, like a Roman Emperor, who was drinking Guinness, the barmaid, who was old and lacquered, the arguing farmers, one of whom had on yellowish, thick-soled shoes, and a bright tie. When my glass was empty, I stared at that.

And my mind got caught then on a kind of mental nail. You can get up, I thought, and walk out, as if nothing had happened. There's nothing to stop you. You can get up, walk out, and go home, as if nothing had happened.

I opened my handbag for a tissue, and little damp marks remained where I had touched the leather. I thought, but if I go now, I may never know what it is she has tried with such care to keep from me.

At the back of my mind, though, remained the refrain: you can get up, walk out of here, just walk out, there is still nothing to prevent it; you cannot do what you are doing, it is intolerable, you are spying.

And there was a point then when the absolute realization came to me that it was true, I couldn't just sit here and wait to spy on her. I accepted it. I got up and walked to the door, sensing eyes on my back.

After that what I saw from the doorway might for me have been some film clip that the projectionist on a whim had speeded up.

I saw a soldier, a sergeant, who had got out of a jeep, walk along the pavement, heavy-footed in his army boots. He looked at me, but I was nothing to him. The first thing I noticed, I think anyone would have noticed about him, was how handsome he was — straight nose, moulded chin, reddish brown complexion. His folded forage cap had been buttoned across one shoulder of his tunic. His hair was thick and black. He must have been well over six feet tall.

He was walking towards Joanna, who had her back to me.

My heart stopped, then began to race. I watched as if mesmerized.

"Jo!" he said, and when he reached her he put his hands on her shoulders, and bent, the khaki against her apricot anorak, to kiss her mouth.

But she averted her face, and, one after the other, returned his hands to his side.

There was a barely perceptible pause before she said, her voice low but quite level, "I just wanted you to know that this time *I'm* ditching *you.*"

I can't clearly recall what followed. I have never been able to, I suppose because of everything I felt, the intensity of it. I know that he looked astonished, and that his expression then was replaced by something that could have been anger, but he controlled himself. He said in a sort of half-murmuring voice something like, "Pack it in, Jo. This is no time for playing games."

When he took her into his arms it wasn't roughly but it wasn't gently either, and though she tried to free herself she couldn't.

I think it was the sight of her being held against her will that finally woke me from my trance. I went up to them.

I don't think I had any physical contact with him at all, I may have, but I don't think I did. He seemed so unprepared for an intervention from any quarter, let alone from me, that he simply released her. I put my arm round her shoulders. "Come on, Joey," I said.

We began to walk away. I don't know where we were walking. Just away. Anyway, anywhere, to leave behind this part of her life. But we couldn't have gone many yards before he caught up with us.

I'm sure I wasn't aware of it at the time, but looking back I see that the questions to which he angrily demanded answers were the questions earlier I had asked. What is all this? What is going on? (Though I suppose he must have asked questions about me, strangely I can't remember that at all.)

But he now was up against a Joanna who had, so to speak, planned her chapter and given herself just one line — which, as far as she was concerned, had said all there was to say: that he had left her high and dry to cope as best she could with the disintegration of their shared adventure. Perhaps, too, what it had said was that there was a teenage pride to rehabilitate.

At any rate, white-faced but resolute, she wouldn't stop to talk to him. And in the end there was nothing left for him but to walk away in his turn.

Quite clearly I remember his last words, "Please yourself," he said. I remember the sound of his boots on the pavement, "If it's a keeper you want!"

We found ourselves wandering in the back streets of Meering, our one purpose to talk. At last was her chance to ask, "Roz, what are you doing here?" And now her voice did shake, and I was struck again by the whiteness of her face.

"It's all right, darling. Joey, it's all right." Oh, I thought, if only you knew how all right it is.

"I know it's all right," she said. "Only I was afraid I wouldn't be able to do it properly."

"Properly?"

"I thought I might swallow in the middle or trip over his feet. I was afraid —"

"You did it marvelously."

"Did I?" She said it rather doubtfully. "But I didn't expect an audience for my performance."

"You shouldn't have had one."

It was at this, then, that we each told our story.

Hers was quite simple. The soldier had contacted Pauline to find out where she was. "I suppose when he thought it had all blown over. Then Pauline wrote to me. So I phoned her. It had to be in a call box for her. I couldn't phone the school. She gave me the time and the number. And we fixed it up."

"However did you know about the Barley Mow?"

"I asked around at school," she said, "for the kind of place Alison wouldn't be seen dead in."

"Darling, how did you get here?" There was a pure wonderful luxury now in being able to ask questions.

"I walked."

"But, Joey, why did *you* have to use a call box?"

"Because I didn't want it to have anything to do with Cassie," she said. "That wouldn't have been fair. Not even on her phone bill, though that wasn't really what mattered. Nothing at all to do with her."

"Why didn't you want it to have anything to do with me?"

I waited.

"I thought you might try and stop me. I thought you would. I thought you'd say, let it go. It's not worth it. It's petty. It's beneath you. And I *had* to do it."

"I'm hardly the one for such a high moral line. Taking bits of paper out of dustbins."

"Neither of us. Neither of us models of how to behave. Actually," she added, "I didn't think you'd do that. I thought it was safe once it was in the kitchen. But I'm glad. It shows you really cared about me."

"Of *course* I really care about you."

We looked at each other. We were passing a rather dispiriting housing estate. I suppose it was odd, but rarely had I felt happier; it was the happiness of relief, and of a relationship that seemed to have moved somehow on to deeper territory.

"What shall we do now?"

She took hold of my wrist and though she was wearing her own watch, turned my watch towards her, the natural intimacy of the gesture an absolute pleasure to me. "We could go to the pictures," she said. For the first time then she smiled, the familiar smile that was almost a laugh.

* * * * *

When we left the cinema there was something about the light that suggested to me winter would soon be on its way out.

TWELVE

I woke to find her sitting on the edge of my bed. She was in her dressing gown, and she was stroking my hair.

"Joanna, what's the matter?"

"Nothing."

"What's the time?" I saw her with astonishment, and delight.

"Two-ish. I was just lying in bed thinking about you, and so wanted us to be together," she said. "I was thinking how great it is that William likes your book, and how much I liked the first one, and how I can't wait to read this one. William isn't the right name for a publisher. He ought to be a Raoul. Or at least a Mark."

"Would Francesca do?" I sat up, and shook the sleep from me. "There is a Francesca."

"Francesca would be lovely. I was thinking that writing a book must be a bit like riding Barbary. You have to control him when he doesn't really want you to but you have to keep in with him, too."

"You *have* been doing a lot of thinking."

"Haven't I?" She laughed.

"Shhh. Should we be doing this? Well, I've never ridden Barbary, thank God. But it sounds very recognizable."

She nodded, thoughtfully. Then she said, "I saw Mrs. Carnaby's father today. He was mending something for Cassie. I felt like asking him if he'd seen me in Meering."

"Perhaps you shouldn't."

"No, I know. But it is odd, isn't it? We practically put on an amateur dramatic show in Meering and no one seems to notice. Two minutes in a call box, though, and it's public property. You know, I didn't even think of Mrs. Carnaby living in Meering. I don't seem much of a conspirator."

"I'm glad you're not." I had to put my hand inside the fleecy camel dressing gown for the joy, simply, of touching her breasts. "Joey, does your mother know about —?"

"About Steve?" She shook her head. "My father never writes to my mother. And I don't want to. Not about that. One day I'll tell her. She'll understand."

"Poor Steve."

"Oh, come on, Roz, you know that's not true."

"Well it just happens to feel like it at the moment."

"I so want to be with you at night again. Roz, if you do that don't expect me to be sensible." She paused. "Is anyone coming at Easter I could give my bed to?"

"I haven't heard."

"So I don't want it to be Easter. Everyone on holiday."

I imagined then that I caught the sound of Hugh moving in his sleep. I withdrew my hand.

She hesitated a moment, then she stood up. "Good night, darling Roz," she said.

"Good night, Joey. See you tomorrow."

It was when I thought she had gone that she returned to the doorway, saying very softly, "My friends were right, though, weren't they? I only saw the outside of it but I don't think the Barley Mow would suit Alison."

*****

That was certainly true. Alison's favorite pub was hardly a pub at all. More a hotel really. The Wrayford Arms.

The Sunday she invited us there for lunch to tell us, as it turned out, about *The Gold Digger,* presented something of a problem to Hugh. He liked being with James and Alison, he liked being with Joanna, who had said she must stay at home and work, and he wanted to accept the invitation from his new school friend to spend the whole day with him. In the end his friend won, perhaps because this was breaking new ground, since Tom had died.

It was the kind of hotel where even Roger wore a suit.

Cassie and I had long ago abandoned any idea of trying to match Alison's hospitality, if only because she didn't want us to. She liked to be the one who did the entertaining.

She settled elegantly into her thickly cushioned, low-backed hotel lounge armchair. Dark dress. Not a beautiful silver hair out of place. Roger lit her cigarette. She didn't smoke a lot, never when she was working, but she seemed to want cigarettes when she was on edge or when, as now, she felt luxurious.

"The fulfillment of a materialistic dream," Roger said.

"Thank you, darling. I seem to be nearly out of these, don't I? Still, I believe there's another packet under the dashboard. What dream was that?"

"The plush, the Martini, the Rover round the corner, the tycoon up your sleeve —"

"No tycoon," she said, not displeased. "I am a devoted wife —"

"James, James, Alison, Alison —" I said, having been brought up on A. A. Milne.

"— and a reasonably devoted mother, considering. Though I confess there have been moments when I have not been altogether blind to the advantages of when they are very young."

"Well done," Cassie said. It began to seem that everyone had been brought up on Milne.

"Quick as a flash," Peter said, "down on it like a hawk. Not a literary allusion that passes her by. Not even ones from a rival firm."

"She has no *rivals,*" said James.

"Merely, as you might say, valued colleagues," Alison said. "Roger, dear, it's only now that I seem to have got a really good look at you."

"Yes?" he said.

"And I have to say," she said, "you do look extremely nice."

"For an anarchist," Peter said, laughing at her.

"Are anarchists allowed any materialistic dreams?" I asked.

"I wouldn't know." Roger looked at me with his charming smile. "I have a few. Not too many, or you can't call your soul your own. But I suppose it doesn't do to be too foolishly possessive about one's soul. Are you possessive about yours?"

"I don't think I can be. Very."

"Anyhow, I won't have any objection to the odd paternal acre when the time comes."

"Well, keep it weeded," James said, adding, "Now there's something finds my back out these days."

As they began to talk about backs, Roger said to me, "A pity Joanna's not here. She'd have been on to Pope's paternal acre. How do you think she'll do with her A Levels? I heard Sylvia Hallam saying she was relying on B grades."

"I think she'll do very well."

"She's a funny girl though, Roz, isn't she? I mean, you feel there's more to her than meets the eye. She hasn't got all her goods in the shop window, as you might say."

I didn't answer.

"Speaking personally, I haven't got anywhere with her. Half a step forward and two steps backward."

"Anywhere?"

"And that doesn't mean what you think it means. I really just don't know what to make of her."

"Well, she wants to get good exam results. Roger, are we here just as a treat or is there some purpose of Alison's behind it?"

"I'm sworn to secrecy," he said, "until at least the main course."

However, it was the fish stage when, glancing up from the neat dissection of her lobster, Alison said, "My dears, by the way, there is something I have to propose. Our health, I shouldn't wonder. We all work far too hard. We all need a break. A change of scene. And what I'm wondering is this — how would a leisurely sail along the French coast strike you? A general eye on Biarritz, say. Though the last thing we would want is to be shackled to a plan."

We looked at her.

"In consideration of certain financial arrangements my friend Bill Moon and I have been able to arrive at, he is prepared for the duration of ten days or thereabouts to give us his services and lend us his boat."

"Good God!" Cassie said.

Peter had begun to smile.

"I have found Mr. Moon in my dealings with him an accommodating man —"

"Easy-going as money," Roger remarked.

"— and there are really only two conditions he has put forward on his side. One is that, should you be interested, we embark on this trip — a maximum of mental refreshment, as I see it, and a minimum of tiresome travel — the moment the schools break up for the summer. The other relates to his status on board as captain. We need not concern ourselves with such matters as lowering the ensign when he is ashore. But he tells me, and is very firm on this point, that the captain has a cabin to himself."

"Always," Peter agreed.

"Now as I believe I did mention to you, Peter, there are three double cabins and three singles. So if our little party were made up as I would hope, this would present no problem. You and Cassie, and your protégé, if she wanted to join us, since I imagine you wouldn't wish to leave her to her own devices while she awaits the results of her scholastic labors. Roz and Hugh. I doubt that Hugh will say no. And Roger has been designated second mate. James," she added, smiling at her husband, has expressed a preference for a Spey-side fishing holiday."

"It is true," James said.

"Oh, come on, you come with us, too," said Peter — thus, though James shook his head, being the first effectively to say "count me in."

"Between now and then," Alison went on, "certain work is being put in hand. Space economy, for example. Plain but stylish is to be the watchword. With a bit of Old English thrown in. That reminds me, I must mention to Bill there's to be an auction at Wrayford Manor some time in the Easter holidays. His objective is the American market. Those rich enough to have grown tired of the luxury cruise." She paused while waiters cleared away, and brought the next course. "Then there's to be a new engine. I fully agree with this. The present speed, he tells me, is around six knots and he needs to improve on that. Everything else, it appears, is fine. *The Gold Digger* has been admirably maintained. There's just the little matter of that name."

"The name?" Cassie queried.

"Well, it might have done well enough when a certain type of young man was the owner. But I would have thought it was the last idea you wanted to put into the minds of potential customers."

"What about *The Bountiful Lady?*" Peter suggested.

"There is such a thing," Alison said, "as going too far in the other direction," and she laughed.

"*Circe,*" said Roger.

"*Circe* would be lovely."

"But would you remember how to pronounce it?" she asked me. "I'm not sure I would. However there is time for the matter of the name. That's really up to Bill, anyway, of course. To deal with more mundane matters — our only expenses would be victuals, as I believe the sea-faring term has it, and such toy money as we cared to fritter away on foreign soil. Well, Roz, what do you think?"

I said, "I am speechless."

And I was, with all that that implied. And I thought, I wonder what Hugh will say. But then I thought, as I drank my coffee, I wonder what the arrangements for the cabins would be.

THIRTEEN

"Sod quotes," Joanna said as she saw me open my kitchen window. "I'm not going to quote anything when I grow up." It was Easter Monday. She was in the garden where she had been walking about reading; but now she aimed her book, a low, level throw, rather the kind where you can make pebbles bounce on water, at the wooden table some distance away. It landed with a small scraping sound. "What are you doing?"

"I'm making a cake."

She nodded. "Oh. Where's Hugh?"

"He's watching television. He's been trying to make Peter take him fishing, but they've got friends coming later."

"Yes, I know."

"Anyway, he mustn't bother people. And James has promised to take him some time this week."

"I could take him to the playground now if he wants," she said.

"I'm sure he'll want."

"It reminds me of where my mother used to take me when we lived in Bristol. We called it the rec. It was —" She looked for the word. "— unspectacular, too."

Hugh was down in the garden in an instant, and I watched them go off together. Suddenly she turned and looking up at me said, "I'd like to get him his life jacket."

Hugh's whole day visit to his new friend had in the event proved rather much. He had complained that I had been too late fetching him, and on the way home, to my surprise, had been tearful.

When we had met Peter, Alison's proposal no doubt fresh in his mind, Peter had said, "Come on, Hugh. What would Captain Moon think if he knew that his third mate was crying?"

After that, of course, I had no choice but to explain the whole story on the spot — with the result that Hugh, tears forgotten, was practically out of his mind with excitement.

So that when Joanna had said, "Couldn't we just stay at home and let them all go?" it had been too late — not, so to speak, even up for discussion.

She had seen that. How serious she had been, if at all, I hadn't been sure. She had almost at once made a joke of it. "Perhaps *we* could go, and persuade them all to stay here," she said. "Couldn't we tell them Biarritz is overrated?"

"I think Biarritz is to be a direction rather than a definite port of call."

"Well, where could we say is overrated?"

"Arcachon?"

"*Arcachon?*" She laughed. "Arcachon sounds *wonderful.* Nobody would believe us. We'll just all have to go."

"Don't you really want to?"

"Of course I want to if you're going."

She had sent a note to Alison, thanking her. It was the one definite thing she had done when her exams were over.

Cassie and Mrs. Hallam and the other teachers at school were simply assuming that, though she was leaving late, she would find a place to go to university. This, in their eyes, was what the intelligent girls did.

Her father had twice written to her urging her to read English with a view to teaching. To all this she had simply replied that she would just see what grades she got and then it would be easier to make up her mind.

To me, when we had been talking about it, she had said, "I wouldn't really mind what degree I did. So long as I was near you. I mean, if it was interesting and I was up to it. But you know, Roz, I never could decide things months in advance." And then she had said something which had seemed to me strange at the time, but seems less strange to me now. "Of course, Roz, there are people who do live their lives. But I sometimes have the feeling life is going to live me."

*****

I rescued her Jane Austen from the garden table and experienced an odd pleasure at having it for a little while in my possession.

The afternoon that James, as he had promised, took Hugh fishing I put petrol in my car. It could hardly be more obvious, I suppose, that many things have got better and nicer since the 'fifties, but not everything has. To know that I only have to think of the Riley Tom and I had bought.

It was a rather long, low car, the bonnet longish. Its color was like a mix of bronze and gray, and the surface gave the impression of matte single-color mosaic. The inside was leather and wood and retained a slight smell of natural materials. There were headlamps mounted on the wings. I was about to return it to the garage when Joanna came up to me.

"Roz, where have you been?" she said.

I told her.

"I've been looking for you. I was looking for you by the stream."

I smiled at her. "So now you've found me. Was it anything special?"

Her direct look didn't flicker. "Where could we go to make love?" she said. "It's been such ages and I so want to."

"They'll be back at school next week."

"But I'm not talking about next week. I'm talking about now."

"This very minute?" I hesitated, looking at her. She pushed back her dark hair. She was wearing the same raincoat she had had on when I first saw her. "What's Cassie doing?"

"She's making a cake. Doesn't anyone in this house ever do anything but make cakes?"

"Well, you should know."

She laughed at this. "When you said that it sort of made me jump," she said. "I mean — well, you know what I mean. As if you'd touched me." There was a pause. Then, as though she, standing there by the car, had just thought of the possibility, which I believe she had, she said, "Couldn't we take your car? People do. Make love in cars, I mean. Have you ever?"

"No. Have you?"

She shook her head. "You know I've ever only made love with you." I knew what she meant, and didn't contradict her. "But 'never before' isn't an argument. There can always be a first time."

I hesitated again. "Where would we take it? You mean drive into a wood somewhere? Something like that? I don't know of any woods where we could do that."

"You could think of somewhere."

I was silent.

"Roz, I need you."

"All right," I said, then.

Briefly, she gave me a hug. "Darling Roz. I'll go and tell Cassie. I'll say we've got brain fatigue and we need some fresh air."

I think everyone had simply assumed that, living in the same house, Joanna and I would have become friends, and certainly there was no need even as a courtesy to account for our casual comings and goings. But whether from temperament or upbringing she had a kind of generosity in such matters.

When she came back I had already reversed the car. She got in beside me. After we had driven a little way she said, "I know how Barbary must have felt being let out at the end of the winter. Where are we going?" As she spoke she had put a hand on my knee with the unthinking intimacy which had become a part of our being alone together and which always delighted me.

I knew now where we were going, rather in the way perhaps that ideas come to you when you are writing to a deadline; because they have to. "You'll see," I said.

Wrayford Station was almost half a mile off the Wrayford Road at the point where the road took a right bend that led on in to the town. It had been one of the first country stations to be axed, probably because of its inconvenient position. The day I went there with Joanna was cool and cloudy.

But the last time I had seen Wrayford Station in use it had been a very hot day in June. The occasion remained clear and detailed in my mind; after all, I had known the station's days were numbered. I had gone simply for a last look.

If I thought about it I could see its name, white on black, or maybe the other way round, but bold, curiously defiant, the shelter throwing a spiked shadow onto the platform — the slatted seats, with blistering paint; still, the geraniums in tubs. I don't like geraniums. I think they are cruel flowers. But certainly they were bright.

I could hear the collapsing sound of the signal. The train would arrive with its mane of smoke blown backwards, and for a minute or two there would be a little commotion.

On the day I was thinking about, the poplars that edged the station yard had been a deep green against the remorseless blue of the sky. But without discord — I have always been struck by how the natural world can get away with any color combination.

However, when we arrived now they were barely defined against the thickening cloud. I drove into the yard, my wheels crunching on the gravel, and drew up by them. The station was derelict, deserted.

With our arrival and the stopping of the car something, not embarrassment, but rather like it, an unease perhaps, overtook us. For the second time we talked about stations.

"It's lovely," she said, "in a sad sort of way. What made you think of it?"

"I suppose you did."

What followed was a strange, brief little episode, over, it seemed, almost before it had begun, yet revealing.

We pushed the front seats forward, and she hung her raincoat on one of them. The back seat seemed cold and springy and unfamiliarly small. I think I would have been nearer laughter than in fact I was had she looked less intense and young.

We held hands, kissed; then within the limitations of our situation we began to caress each other, and quite soon the response in me I wouldn't have counted on grew, took over, though more, I am sure, from the warm feel of her than from anything that was done.

I was, I suppose, slow, perhaps because of the different circumstances, to latch on to the absence of a response in her; but I was just doing so when she suddenly said in an anxious voice, "I don't think this is going to work for me, Roz."

Surprised, and not wanting to stop, I said, "Is there something you want me to do that would make it better?"

"No. That would make it worse. It doesn't feel like making love. Not coming here specially, like this. It just feels like doing things. It —"

Sitting up, I resisted the temptation to say, well, it was your idea.

"I know it was my idea. I thought it would be all right. Roz, I'm sorry."

"It is all right." I laughed, and shrugged. "Nothing ever always works. And we have forever."

"I'm sorry," she said again.

"It doesn't matter." I buttoned her shirt. "Come on, let's go back."

"I didn't want to pretend."

"No."

It was when I had slowed down for the T-junction at the Wrayford Road that she said, "Cuddle me, Roz."

"This very minute?" I remembered saying that before.

"Yes."

I pulled the car slightly off the small, almost unused road.

"Should I turn on the lights? It looks at though it could thunder."

"No one will hit us here."

I put my arm round her, and she leaned against me, our faces close.

"It *was* sad, wasn't it?" she said. "The station. Ghost sad. That little boarded-up office, and no one in it. I'd like to have seen it when it was real."

"I think I have a sort of passion for little branch-line stations," I said. "I store them up in my mind. Perhaps against the day when there won't be any left."

"But you aren't sad about us? Don't be, Roz. In a way it's almost worth it, making us know how wonderful it mostly is. Truly know, I mean."

I touched her face.

"And you won't be sad now every time you come in the car?"

"No, Joey, I won't. I might want to laugh."

"Then I'll never forgive you. Did you keep this car because of Tom?"

"I really don't know why I kept it. I could get some that would be cheaper to run. But I just don't want to. I'd rather use it less."

"Let's start a petrol pool. My mother's car was a Singer. While she was here. She bought it without telling my father. Once one Sunday afternoon she and I did over eighty in it." I could hear the approach of a car from Wrayford. "Just for the —"

As it rounded the bend, its headlights swept across us, then the car, a Rover, was gone, on its way in the direction of Whitethorn. By some kind of tacit agreement we didn't change our position; I kept my arm round her.

"That was Alison," she said. "She had furniture in the back. Little tables or something. Did you see?"

"Yes. Oh yes. There was an auction at Wrayford Manor. She's probably been to that. I don't think you were there when she mentioned it. She —"

Momentarily we had avoided what was in our minds. But then Joanna said, "Will she make some great story out of it? Seeing us here?"

"If she did see us. I don't know."

"But you know Alison."

"I'm not sure that I do, really. And, anyway, this is — well, there's hardly been any kind of rehearsal."

"I don't want her to spoil it. Could she?"

"I suppose she could make it difficult. Though why would she want to? Would it matter very much to you?"

"Not for me." There was a long pause. "People do spoil what's beautiful. And it *is*, Roz. Beautiful that we don't want anything from each other, that we're not *for* anything. That we're just in love. Have you really thought?"

"Of course I've thought."

"What about *The Gold Digger?*" she said, suddenly.

"Perhaps nothing about *The Gold Digger*. And not even *The Gold Digger* can govern our lives. I won't invent things, for Alison or anyone else."

"What sort of things?"

"I suppose we could say you were feeling sick, anything. But I won't. Would you?"

"No. I love you."

I turned on our lights. "Look, Joey. One thing. There's nothing anybody in the world could ever do or say could make me change about you." I switched on the engine and put the car into gear.

*****

James brought Hugh home. For several days after that neither Joanna nor I saw Alison though it would be silly to pretend that we didn't think about her. Cassie, who had seen her, merely remarked that she was at last thinking of installing a lift. "She says keeping fit's all very well, but not if it kills you."

I made no comment.

How far it was conscious I'm not sure but it seems to me now that in those days when I was wondering about Alison I adjusted my attitude to the people around me, except of course for Hugh and Joanna herself. I think my purpose was to convey a detachment, the message that my life was my own and only mine.

I did it, I think, even to Roger. He called 'round about the tortoise. I was just going out and we met on the doorstep. Hugh and I had had a grass snake living with us for a very short time. It lay on grass in a biscuit tin and refused the food we had got from the pet shop. In the end we took it to some woodland and let it go. It escapes me who gave it to Hugh. Probably one of Cassie's pupils. I am entirely clear who gave him the tortoise. It was Mrs. Carnaby.

If there was one thing I learned from the incident of the tortoise it was that sometimes people's actions are so inexplicable you simply have to accept them and not try to explain. The intention was kind, and I remember being touched by it, but the truth is, there isn't a lot a little boy can do with a tortoise that would be appreciated, or for that matter, I suppose, with a grass snake, and, anyway, the tortoise had hibernation in mind.

Roger said, "I found it by the stream. It must have got through a hole in the fence, though I couldn't see one. I've put it back."

"Thank you, Roger."

"It seemed very single-minded. It was probably making straight for our lettuce. Not that I care for lettuce. Do you care for tortoises?"

"I haven't given it a great deal of thought. I suppose they have a certain decrepit charm. Roger, I must go."

"There's a writer's line if ever there was one."

"Not a very good one. 'Decrepit' isn't the right word. I *must* go. Hugh's coming out early. The school has got people away ill."

"Is Joanna anywhere around?" he said.

"Cassie's showing her how to knit."

"*Knit?* Cassie's at home, is she?"

"Yes. I don't know why. Roger, see you."

I could have told him more of the story, but I didn't. I could have told him, for instance, that having worked herself almost to a standstill with her exam revision Joanna had said in a moment of pure indulgent fantasy that she would knit Hugh's teddy a cravat. I could have told him the reason for the cravat was that the teddy's head had come loose and my attempts to tighten it showed. Moreover, they hadn't been very successful.

It was a not very big teddy, well-worn, with mesmeric, rather drugged-looking button eyes. It spent most of its time in pajamas which were also well-worn and had once caused Peter, who didn't very often make jokes, to say it looked as if it had seen better nights. But Hugh was not ready to abandon it.

He was six. Though as he came out of school his blazer, the gray shorts, the sturdy shoes made him seem grown up for a teddy, which was why I had put it in a paper bag, I knew there were still times when he wasn't.

We went together to the little antique shop a few doors away from James's bank. The antique dealer's wife ran a dolls' repair service. What happened when we came out of the shop, for all its near farce, curiously underlined what I had already learned — that to be suddenly and totally surprised by life is in fact a commonplace.

We were in time for only the tail end of what had been going on in the bank and which created such a stir in Whitethorn, became such a subject of conversation, though less than a decade later it probably wouldn't have rated banner headlines even in the local press.

There was a woman standing nearby with a Columbine carrier bag who in due course explained to the small crowd that quickly gathered what had happened. "He just ran in and shouted something and jumped over the counter. They'll have to do something about that counter. Then he hit him and took the money and tried to get away. But he wasn't quick enough."

All I saw was the boy running out. If he had ever had anything over his face he no longer had it. He reminded me in a curious way of the boys Joanna and I had seen at the Juvenile Court, but a few years on. He had some sort of weapon in his hand, I didn't see exactly what. Immediately following him was a cashier I knew quite well, a young man who yawned a good deal, as if permanently in need of a sound night's sleep. But he wasn't yawning now. He had the expression of someone who had been altogether too provoked.

Two more cashiers came out of the bank, and James, who had taken off his gold-rimmed spectacles.

When the first cashier caught up with the boy he wrestled him to the ground, and taking him by the hair, bumped his head twice on the pavement, not so much forcibly as indignantly.

As I watched them it passed bizarrely through my mind that they were like schoolboys who were becoming too rough and that what was needed was for the teacher who had produced Mrs. Hallam's scenes from *Twelfth Night* to say in peremptory tones, "Stop this silliness at once."

However, for an instant Hugh was the only person to speak. Reverting to a construction of earlier years he said, "Why did that man do that for?"

Then everybody began to talk — and Whitethorn went on talking about it for days.

* * * * *

But when the next morning Alison and I met in the street she didn't talk about it at all. She was with Bill Moon. She crossed over the road to me.

"Roz, I wanted to see you." Then, without explaining her words further, and making, I think, the shortest speech I ever head her make, she said, "If being happy comes your way, be happy. It's one thing none of us can ever organize."

FOURTEEN

It was subsequently clear, or so it seemed to me, that that was as far as Alison wanted to go. She had nailed a small color to her mast representing the goodwill of a friend, but I am sure she had no wish for spoken certainties, still less for attempts to bridge the gulf in understanding which for her, I have no doubt, must have been considerable.

On my part, though I confess I was thankful not to have to face a chain of personal and unpredictable reactions, there was a reluctance to have her, so to speak, in any sense within the private circle of my relations with

Joanna. As a result for a time our contacts became more superficial and fewer.

Joanna and I during the month or so before she took her exams kept to our work plan, and regularly made love, though we avoided drawing any particular attention to ourselves.

*****

Considering the whimsical nature of the English climate, it is remarkable how June examinations more or less always take place in a spell of weather perfectly designed to give hay fever sufferers a rough ride.

Joanna didn't have hay fever but by the end of her final paper she was restless, on edge, didn't want to discuss any of the papers, and on the day immediately following we decided to go together to Stainton.

It was like the kind of day when for no real reason I had said goodbye to a functioning Wrayford Station — immensely hot, and the sun safely in a sky without cloud.

The first thing we did when we arrived was go to the ships' chandler near the harbor to get Hugh his life jacket, for which she had made meticulous measurements. Having put it in the car, we wandered over to where we had first seen *The Gold Digger.* The yacht was no longer there. I knew through Alison Bill Moon had taken charge. Where Bill and the yacht were now I had no idea. I only knew that next month we were to go aboard at Southampton for our holiday, and that in the meantime the name was to be changed. Bill had wanted *Ocean Woman,* but Alison had decreed that this was not securely commercial enough. They had settled for *The Golden Plover.*

I didn't know whether this was a particularly good name or not. I felt that it was neither here nor there to me, anyway. So far as I was concerned the yacht was likely to remain *The Gold Digger* in my mind. I think changing names is difficult. It can be with writing, I have found. Characters seem very soon to take over their names, and however convenient a change might be, their names tend simply to have become their names, and that's it.

Joanna said, "I'd have called her *Horizon.* Come on, Roz, let's get our picnic."

We bought ham rolls, and fruit, and some milk and walked for about half an hour by the edge of the sea, the beach gradually becoming emptier as we walked, and within ten minutes we were alone. At length we reached the cluster of half a dozen rocks that marked the effective end of that part of the beach. The rocks were shaped like the leafy part of a poplar tree, though they weren't as high. We changed into swim suits.

"Are you going in?"

She stood tossing from hand to hand some pebbles she had picked up, hesitating. Then she threw the pebbles, one after another, hard, at the sea, still undecided.

If there was a clue to the future in her moon of that day, I didn't pick it up. Finally she said, "No, I don't think I will. I'll just get hotter and hotter. What about you?"

I shook my head.

We had our picnic between two of the larger rocks.

"Hardly Alison's style," she said. "Do you remember how she went on about drying off in the sun or something? When we were here and it rained and rained."

"Yes, I remember."

"Alison *is* amazing. I think about what she said to you. About being happy. I'm not sure I would have expected it from her."

"I'm not sure I would. I think about it."

"You know that time Cassie was supposed to be teaching me to knit and Roger came and interrupted? I don't know what we were talking about but he said then Alison sometimes surprises even him."

"We've begun to say 'do you remember?' "

"Well, we've known each other a long time." She finished the apple she was eating, and threw the core away. "I suppose I shouldn't have done that. Still, it'll rot. Or make a plover happy. I'd rather be a tern. Free as an Arctic tern making for the sun. Do you know, they actually do fly hundreds of thousands of miles. They really do. Oh, look, Roz."

She had noticed a small pink flower growing at the base of one of the rocks. Its petals seemed a cross between a pink and a poppy. I don't think I had seen a flower like it before.

She went over and knelt down by it, touching it gently. "It doesn't smell."

She returned to where she had been sitting.

"When I was about Hugh's age, younger," she said, "I went to a party and stole one of those pink roses on the birthday cake. I put it in water when I got home and it melted. My mother bought me a whole bunch of real ones. Tell me something about when you were little."

I had to think. "I hated circuses."

"But you didn't have to go to circuses, did you?"

"I went to one. I hated the animals being made to do things, and I didn't like the music, and I was afraid someone would fall off the wires, and I didn't even think the clowns were funny. I was a dead loss."

"*It* was a dead loss."

She ran a hand up my leg. Already as she spoke again she was slipping her shoulder straps over her arms. "I don't want this on," she said. "There isn't anyone for miles. And, anyway, it's petty. A littleness of people against the rest of it here. Without our clothes we're a part of the universe."

"It's a good line, Joey."

"It feels marvelous." She was lying back on the hot sand, luxurious, her arms under her head.

Naked, it did feel marvelous. Indulged. Uncluttered.

After a while I slightly parted her legs so that I could lie between them, propped on my elbows, looking at her, knowing that soon we would make love, in some odd way enjoying the postponement.

I thought, I don't know the words, untrite words, for being precisely true about the desire her nakedness effortlessly starts in me. It has above all to do with her, Joanna, Joanna in her head, yet to do, too, with some strange sensual force the generalized idea of mouth, breasts, hips can deploy.

It had so crucially to do with the mysterious magic center of her pleasure, which on impulse, changing my position, I covered with my hand.

I suppose I have never believed that one human being can possess another, not really. We belong only to ourselves. But that late morning in the sun I had the feeling that, incredibly, wonderfully, she was mine — that "Let me . . ." was no part of it, that anything from love I could want to do would be allowed, welcomed, responded to.

"What are you thinking?"

"That somebody wrote about 'love flesh.' It's nice, but somehow it's — oh, I don't know, passive."

"Like your Riley without its engine."

"Like that exactly. Who wrote it?"

She shook her head.

"Do you know — did I ever tell you? — that just sometimes I can feel the throbbing inside you."

She laughed softly. "I'm not surprised." Then she pulled me onto her, drawing me down with her arms so that we were close against each other, moving, she was kissing my mouth, saying against it, "I love you" . . . and we made love, with passion, and a new abandon.

When it was over, the taste of her on my tongue, my whole consciousness suffused with the faint, marvelous smell of her skin, the feel and touch of her, we lay silent on the sand.

Until at last she said, the low-pitched voice now so quiet that it was almost as if she was talking to herself, "Roz, if I didn't love you I would love you for that."

No doubt it is in the nature of being in love to be subjectively (not to say perhaps tediously, for others) entranced by, for instance, voice, smile, words spoken, and it could be that something of that subjectivity reaches out to me still; but I do believe I am objective in my recollection of her beauty that day.

We got dressed then, and walked over the firm damp sand by the sea back to the car.

We drove home very fast, which she liked, to be in time to collect Hugh. Descending one of the hills on the way, I misjudged the speed of a farm vehicle and was obliged to overtake it, missing by only yards an oncoming car.

"Christ Almighty," Joanna said. "Roz, be careful. Don't kill us. Not when everything feels as if it's just beginning. At least don't do it for them."

I knew what she meant. Though we didn't often talk about the threat which, comparatively new at that time, hung over the world, when we did, as I recall, it was with little enough presence. We could not but be aware of it.

She ruffled my hair.

That evening, both of us tired and hungry, we took Hugh to one of the cafés in the town for something to eat.

She remarked that her mother's favorite sauce was Créole.

FIFTEEN

Cassie took an interest in a particular Third World charity and was proposing to have a garden fête for raising money. One evening a group of us sat on the grass discussing plans for this.

Summer had possessed the garden. Flowers chosen for their scent, blossoming shrubs, had all come in to their own, the yews by the gate were thick and impenetrable with foliage, and midges from the stream dived and circled in the soft, moist air.

Mrs. Carnaby suddenly slapped at her neck. "Everything," she confided to one of Cassie's friends, several of whom were present, "bites me. Doesn't matter what it is, it bites me. Now my dad, nothing bites him. He could pick up a hedgehog and all its little playmates would look the other way. I tell him its just a matter of being a tasty morsel. But what I'm telling you, dear, is there's no justice. No justice at all." She slapped at her neck again.

Whenever it was to do with Cassie Mrs. Carnaby, her bicycle forever at the ready, always helped. And on this occasion she also had another purpose — to forward the interests of her neighbor's son, the one who had moved on from conjuring and puppets to forming his own band.

Her relations with her neighbors were prevalent rather than smooth, but in the case of this boy she did seem to have been rather consistently well-disposed.

As she had in the past explained to me and now explained to everybody there, he wasn't "a bad lad," his mother having had the sense to keep him "under." "And it might help to get him started," she said, "with his little band, I mean. Playing at Mrs. Turner's fête. Besides, it would be nice for the young ones to have some music. Don't you think?" Nobody disagreed.

I remember only parts of what was said at that gathering, probably because I didn't pay a great deal of attention. I had arranged, at the risk of further comment on the subject from Joanna, that I would make a cake, for anyone interested in such a long shot as trying to guess its weight, and I suppose I felt that that justified me in thinking of other things.

Hugh, for instance. He sat crayoning a book on heraldry. His enthusiasm for this project was largely accounted for, I think, by the fact that the book he had was really too advanced for him, having come from one of the older classes. But he had been allowed all the same to bring it home with him to color. I was glad about the way his attitude to school was changing.

I do recall being somewhat surprised at Joanna's remark that her nuns had been in a class on their own as fund-raisers. "It's all a question of temptation," she had said. "Really tempting prizes to make people part with real money — though only one will win. Basically betting, of course, though you have to wrap it up a bit, in case it's not too legal."

However, James, present to please Cassie in what might be called a fiscal capacity, wasn't happy about any kind of betting, wrapped up or otherwise.

She didn't exactly argue with him. She simply said, politely, mildly even, "Well, I don't think the Third World will get much help from bran tub lucky dips and trying to drop pennies over sixpenses in a bucket of water. And honestly, Mr. Elliott, I never heard of any of the nuns going to prison."

This reference to prison then led to some conjecture on the part of Mrs. Carnaby as the fate of the young man who had attempted, so ludicrously, to raid James's bank.

It was Roger who deflected Joanna towards the idea of side-shows for children — on the principle that "kids and their money" were soon parted. "What kinds of things do kids like doing?" he asked.

"Hair-raising things," she said. "Perhaps we could rig up something for them to climb."

"What do you mean, climb?"

"Oh, the usual thing. Ascend. Gain height."

I remember being struck by how, temporarily, with Roger she could sometimes seem to revert to the Senior Schoolgirl. But he, on the other hand, seemed to me over the past weeks to have become somehow less of a boy.

"Perhaps we could build something sensationally high," she was suggesting, extemporizing now, no longer serious, "and let them jump off into a barrel, say. That must be quite exciting."

He laughed. "Or once 'round the field on Barbary. And your money back if you make it."

But she said then, her tone changing, "They really *are* thinking of selling Barbary."

Hugh looked up from his crayoning. Mrs. Carnaby saw this and smiled at him, and afterwards at me.

"By the way, Mrs. Taylor, dear," she said, "I've been thinking. If there's going to be a lot of comings and goings with this fête we'd better take the tortoise upstairs for the duration. We want," she added, "to be fair to the child," lowering her voice. "We don't want that tortoise of his lost or trodden on. Now let me see, it's the day after tomorrow, isn't it, I'm to collect his Lordship?"

"Yes, Mrs. Carnaby," I said.

Upstairs later, Hugh continued with his crayoning. As he worked, he said, "Was Daddy like a knight?"

"He was very nice."

"Who do you love most in the world now?"

"Who do you think?"

"I love Barbary. Why can't Joanna buy Barbary?"

"Well, how could she look after him when she's at university?" Despite myself my heart did sink a little as I said the words. But he had returned to his new interest, giving a final touch here and there to the coats of arms, and then holding them up for me to see. "La bel —" he read slowly.

"Crescent."

"Now read these."

I read, "Molet, Martlet, Annulet. You've done them very nicely."

"Yes," he agreed. He paused. "I don't really want the tortoise up here."

"No, but Mrs. Carnaby thought it would be best. And she did give the tortoise to you."

"Why is she going to collect me?"

"Because I'm going to have lunch with William."

* * * * *

William had invited me to lunch, I think, because he was quite pleased with the sales of the first novel, which had been rather larger than he had expected, and certainly larger than I had, and also because he seemed to feel the second one might have surmounted the notorious hurdle of all second novels. Also, perhaps, to give me encouragement for getting on with the next.

But the reason for his high good humor was that his firm, against serious opposition, had acquired some war memoirs which were clearly going to make them a fortune.

He took me to a restaurant in Thorn Street much frequented by publishers and their guests. It was large, very light, with areas of glass roof. I subsequently went there on various occasions and more than anything associate it with people who knew one another exchanging greetings from table to table.

"Now, Roz," he said, "let's make a splendid meal of it. What do you suppose might take your fancy?"

He was a tall, thin man of probably nearer sixty than fifty, with gray hair brushed back, who habitually wore formal clothes, but perhaps because he stooped a lot his suits always looked as though they had never been pressed. That day his cheerfulness was almost palpable.

"William, have you ever heard of Créole sauce?"

"Créole sauce? Créole sauce? Of course I have. Excellent with sole. Is that what you're in the mood for? Perhaps I could organize it. If you're not in any particular hurry. I seem to recall it's made with sherry. But I could be wrong."

Such was the size of his account with the restaurant that he managed without too much difficulty to organize the Créole sauce. As he did everything else to do with the meal.

He talked at first a great deal on the subject of the war memoirs, this obviously being the thing nearest to his heart. At one stage, when briefly he was called to the telephone, I found myself thinking, in a kind of aside, a bizarre aside, that had Alison chosen to create a great story about Joanna and me, I would have chosen — having lived through the forties and all they had done to the world — to go to the fête with a badge which asked : AND DO YOU WANT TO MAKE A FUSS ABOUT LOVE?

Only then I recollected Alison saying, I couldn't remember in what connection any more, "Roz, don't be defensive."

Oh well; it was all of it long, long before the reforming movement, the supportive group . . .

When he returned from his telephone call William talked to me about my own writing, methods of going about it, the new book, and so on, and because he was both sympathetic and knowledgeable I think I enjoyed the prolonged lunch more than anything I had done without her since Joanna and I had met.

On the way home in the train, as the black specks of train-smoke dirt on the windows appeared to mark first London suburbs, and then fields and villages most of the way to Whitethorn, I began to my surprise thinking about the talk I would maybe try to do for Mrs. Hallam, since she wanted it.

Then a porter called out Whitethorn's name.

Back home, having picked up the car from the station yard, the first thing I noticed was that the front door was open. I went in, and almost immediately Peter appeared. "Hallo, Roz," he said, but clearly this wasn't what he had to say. He went on at once, "Roz, I'm afraid there's been a bit of an accident."

I looked at him, and waited. I couldn't have come remotely near to guessing what the accident might be, but the word itself creates alarm in all of us.

"It's Hugh," Peter said. "I'm afraid he got thrown off Barbary."

At first I thought I had misheard. "Barbary?" I gazed at him. "Is Hugh all right? I mean he isn't —"

My heart had begun to race.

"No, no," he said. He hesitated. "I got home early and told Mrs. Carnaby it would be O.K. if she went. Hugh was with Joanna. I don't know exactly what happened, but —"

"Peter, where is he now?"

"The hospital. It's a good thing I was here. I was able to drive them in. He wasn't unconscious but he did seem rather knocked about. Joanna's stayed with him. I came back to see you. Cassie's at a staff meeting."

"Thank you," I said mechanically. "I must go to the hospital."

What I said next I suppose was quite irrational. "I'll just get some more money." I didn't really know why I might need money. But I went upstairs, and took some notes from my desk, scarcely noticing at the time that there was a small packet lying on it.

When I returned downstairs Peter said, "Roz, I'd better take you."

"No, Peter, you stay and see Cassie. Is he very bad?"

"We thought somebody should have a look at him. I think I ought to drive you, Roz."

"No, I'll be all right." I went back to the car.

Whitethorn Cottage Hospital was a little way outside the town itself. As soon as I got there I went to Enquiries, and the clerk asked me to wait.

Waiting was terrible. I wanted to know about Hugh at once; I wanted to go to him, only I didn't know where he was. As I stood by the window, with the feeling that to sit might slow things up, I was conscious of the two other women present, who had an air somehow of having been discarded, forgotten. The younger one, the daughter perhaps, was in a tight velvet suit, was heavily made up, with hair a curious bronze except near the roots. At the time I thought nothing about her at all. Now, remembering — and for some reason I remember them so clearly — it seems to me she had the look of a woman who had sought, through her own notion of sexiness, for her own notion of the free life, the sweet life, but hadn't proved cut out for it.

They moved up a little on the bench to make room for me but I thanked them and refused, continuing to look for someone to come about Hugh.

They had with them a small passive-seeming child with plaits who brightened when a nurse came in. Though I wasn't listening I remember her saying, "Give Patsy a sweet to keep Patsy quiet?"

The nurse disregarded this as if she had heard it before and said to me, "The doctor won't be a moment, Mrs. Taylor. He'll see you in just a moment," she repeated.

I don't like hospitals, perhaps in common with a majority of people. At an emotional level I never have liked anything about them. I never wanted a toy nurse's uniform, my dolls were never ill, and never got hurt.

That day, because I was there through Hugh, everything about the hospital seemed even worse: the smell, the little detached, dreadful, frightening smells that branch off from it, the clean brisk atmosphere, the waiting.

When the doctor arrived I said to him, "How is my son?" He proved to be a matter-of-fact Yorkshireman, probably not yet into his thirties, and predisposed, one felt, to a positive attitude.

He said, almost without preliminaries, "Of course, it's shaken him up a bit. You don't fall off a horse and land against a brick wall and feel your best afterwards. But it could have been worse. Given his chest a bit of a thump."

"Badly —?" I had caught my breath.

"Not too bad. No bones broken. The x-rays are clear. And no real damage done. He's been lucky. He's not enjoying himself. But he'll be all right." The doctor gazed a moment at the ceiling. "Now let me see. We'll keep him in for tonight, but I don't see any reason why he shouldn't go home some time tomorrow, though — not after we've given him a last look over. It's mainly a matter of the dope. We thought it best to sedate him."

"I want to see him."

"All right, but you'll find him pretty sleepy."

He handed me over to the nurse, who took me along corridors to a smallish ward where Hugh was lying in a bed in a corner. He looked at me without smiling and without a greeting. There was a reddish dark bruise all down the left side of his face. His hair was black against the whiteness of the pillow.

Joanna was sitting at the end of his bed as, in such different circumstances, I had often seen her do before. She got up when I came in. "Roz —"

I was aware without really noticing that she had on white jeans newly dirt-streaked, and a red long-sleeved shirt.

I went straight to Hugh, and took one of his hands. There was a plaster on it. The nails looked unnaturally dark.

I said, "Darling, are you all right?"

He nodded. His eyes were very big. He didn't seem to want to talk. So I just held both of his hands, then. I wanted to take him into my arms, but I remembered what the doctor had said about his chest.

Joanna didn't speak. It was when I had turned to her and said, "What were you doing?" that the nurse came back and murmured something about only one at a time being best, taking Joanna's arm and quietly persuading her away. At some point, Peter and Cassie came, but they, too, were asked not to stay.

I don't know how long I sat with Hugh. Eventually he went to sleep.

"You should leave him now," the nurse said.

"I don't want to go home."

"I'm afraid we haven't any sleeping arrangements."

"It doesn't matter. Can I just stay here in the waiting room and see that he's all right?"

"Well, if you like. You won't be very comfortable." She added, kindly, "I'll tell the night nurse."

By the door of the ward a young woman I took to be a medical student was sitting at a bed seemingly waiting for the little boy in it to return to consciousness. The child had something like the frame of a pair of earphones, a kind of band, on his head. I didn't know what it was. He gave a small moan and stirred. She watched him closely, her concentration never flagging. I think she was oblivious of everyone. As I passed, she drew the curtains round him. The sight was terrifying to me.

I walked back to the waiting room in a daze of mixed emotions. I remember flowers outside doors, scarlet-blanketed stretchers, an oxygen cylinder, green walls, and dim lights, and the cloudy, unexplained sounds of nursing. All of it separate yet related, like the squares and oblongs of a plaid.

Joanna was standing in the waiting room.

I said, "What happened?" For the second time then I asked, "What were you doing?"

"Roz, I was giving him a ride on Barbary, but —"

"A ride? On Barbary?" I stared at her. "That was crazy. Absolutely senseless. An absolutely stupid thing to do. Barbary isn't a beach donkey."

"No, Roz, that isn't the way it was. He wanted to, he knows Barbary might not be there much longer, he so wanted to, and —"

"What has that got to do with it? You don't let little children do things just because they want to. Or for God's sake there wouldn't be many of them left."

"It would have been all right, only —"

"All *right*?"

"I had him in front of me, and I was holding him, only then Barbary began to trot. Barbary must have sensed that I had the reins differently or something, and Hugh got frightened and struggled, and I couldn't keep hold of him —"

"What did you expect? Hugh's never been on a horse in his *life*."

She was silent. I looked at her. She was very white. The feeling I had then could have swung either way, but my shock and anger had fed on itself and had to go somewhere.

I said, "It might be all right to be young, it might be all right to be silly even, but it isn't all right to be lethal. You could have killed him."

She made a little move as if to say something different but what she said was, "Roz, is there anything I could do that would help?"

"No." I added, "I'm not going home."

She nodded. "I'll stay with you, of course."

"I don't want you to stay, Joanna."

"Please, Roz —"

"I don't want you to stay with me."

She hesitated, then she turned away. She didn't go towards the telephones but walked out of the hospital door. I didn't know how she was going to get home and for that moment, vengefully almost, I didn't care. Afterwards it was something I felt ashamed of. For what it is worth, I remind myself now it was before rapists and muggers came into our calculations.

During the night I went for a little time to Hugh's bedside, sitting on the small chest of drawers, watching him sleep.

The next day I was allowed to take him home. He walked awkwardly as if he were very stiff, but he was now quite cheerful and even prepared to joke about his "wounded soldier" status. "You know," he said, "it wasn't Barbary's fault."

When we got home we talked about what he would like us to go out and buy for him. After much discussion he decided on a speed boat that "you wind up."

Peter and Cassie and Joanna all came up together to see him. Joanna and I spoke — something superficial and meaningless — but I avoided looking at her.

* * * * *

It was much later when I picked up the little packet on the desk. It contained a fountain pen. In minute letters on the clip had been engraved the familiar "J for R."

I tossed it back on to the desk. But realized then that for the first time I was crying.

SIXTEEN

"I have carried out a careful inspection of the wall and it appears to have suffered no damage. So you won't be getting a bill from me."

"Oh, thank you, Alison. That has taken a load off my mind." We both laughed.

"And he's really all right now?"

"Yes, he seems fine. It seems not to have upset him at all."

"Good. Though it's the kind of thing Hugh could have done without."

"He was quite pleased to be going off to school to tell them all about it for 'news hour.' "

"He'll certainly put his classmates in the shade." Alison paused. "So he'll be all right for the boat, Roz?"

"Oh, yes."

"Well — have your drink. You've done the stairs."

She put a drink for me on one of the two small tables she now had in her studio. I guessed they came from the auction, but neither of us mentioned them, though ordinarily we would have done. However, she did go on to say, "By the way — did I tell you — Bill Moon and I had second thoughts about going too strong on the Old England idea for *The Plover*'s refurbishings. Or I did. We've gone for something nice and cosmopolitan and safe. Why, I ask myself, upset any passing Anglophobe. For one thing, they might have a point. And for another, their money's as good as anyone else's. Talking of money, Roz, the lift's going to be put in while we're away. I'm seriously thinking I shall have to mortgage James and Roger to pay for it."

"Well, it will be wonderful to have a lift."

"Oh, but *you* won't use it. You come under the half century line. You'll have to walk. Do you good."

And she lifted her drink to me in some kind of mock salute, and I knew that suddenly, though she remained unprepared to involve herself in a certain possible aspect of my life, our old relations, less by design than by some odd natural process, had clicked back into place.

But nothing like that happened with Joanna in the days that led us to *The Gold Digger*. We had "made up" — I can't think of a different expression — in the sense that we talked, though not about the accident, did things together, such as, for instance, going to the library, even taking Hugh to the playground in Whitethorn; I thanked her for the pen. (She had given a small, dismissive shrug.) I was no longer consciously angry; anger, after all, is for what has been intentional. But we hadn't come together.

Our relationship had to be restored sexually, and she had made no move towards this, and I'm not sure I could have responded had she done so, and I made no move.

I don't understand myself at that time. Perhaps something of how I had felt at what had happened to Tom had got caught up with how I had felt at what could have happened to Hugh. I don't know. Anyway, it was on my side as if some deep well of feeling had got between me and her, keeping us apart. It was both like and not like a period of bereavement when, however senselessly, however pointlessly, sexual joy is ruled out.

There was no bereavement now. The accident had become for Hugh just a good story. And even the fact that Barbary was finally to be sold to a Meering farmer had all at once to compete with his new excited realization that within measurable time, time measurable to a six year old, he would be aboard Bill Moon's yacht.

Yet I couldn't take her into my arms, and say, just, "Joanna —" I thought about her all the time. I thought about her when I was working, and much of what I had written had to be thrown away.

She spent every morning and half the afternoon with Roger helping prepare for Mrs. Hallam's inter-schools sports day, though neither of them would be present for it since in true Hallam style, it was to be held after the schools had broken up and so after the day appointed for our departure on *The Gold Digger.*

That day came — for James, metaphorically garlanded in his fishing tackle, to wave us bon voyage.

* * * * *

Though the idea of it had been in my mind on and off since Alison had made her proposal, actually being on board I found gave me at first a curious sense of unreality. Walking about the deck, looking at the diversity of boats all around us, blown by a wind already unexpectedly strong, I couldn't help the feeling not only that all of it really had nothing much to do with me but — and this came as a surprise — that in the event I wasn't particularly interested.

"Roz."

I glanced round. It was Cassie.

"Roz, have you seen the galley? There isn't just a coke boiler for the hot water, there's a *bath* down there, too! They've tucked it away very cleverly. Come and have a look. And it's a nice bath, nice shape. Green."

"All right," I said.

I knew that Peter was looking after Hugh. We came on them having a nautical conversation.

"What is it then, that tack?" Hugh was asking.

"Tack? Oh, coming around at the end of a tack. It's really the art of getting the wind on your side when it's actually against you. Quite a tricky thing to do. You have to know what you're up to."

"I could do it."

"Watch him, Peter," Cassie said, "or he'll have us tied up at Cherbourg for an early lunch."

"What's wrong with that? So long as it *is* Cherbourg."

Cassie laughed, in holiday mood, and took my arm. "Come on. The cabins are nice. Which one is yours?"

"I don't know yet. I haven't seen Alison. I thought I'd have a look 'round first."

"I suppose Hugh will be in with you."

"And Joanna in with Alison?"

"I—"

"Or Alison might rather have you. And Hugh in with Joanna."

"I'd rather have Hugh."

"Well, don't complicate things, Roz. Leave that for your next chapter. Just tell Alison that's what you want."

Don't complicate things, I thought. Just say, *I love you....*

"There's going to be coffee in the saloon for everyone any moment now. Where's Joanna, do you know?"

Joanna was helping Bill Moon carry a crate of bottles down to the galley, watched by the mate, a slender, somehow rather reluctant-seeming young man, who didn't smile much, and whose name was Henry.

Now he was frowning. "Is that the last?"

"One to go."

Henry still frowned.

As well as the competent and tireless sailor he didn't look, he was cook, a good one, if rather set on healthy eating. And he turned out to be possessive about the galley.

"Those crates take up too much room," he said. "And where's the lime juice?"

"It'll be around somewhere. Oh, come on, Henry," Bill said equably, "you know booze always looks more than it is. And let's have that coffee, there's a good chap, or we'll miss the tide."

"Coffee," Joanna said. "Great."

The bath *was* nice.

As we went to the saloon I heard her saying to Bill, "Is she difficult to sail?"

"She's not easy. You have to get the hang of it."

"Can I have a try?"

He looked at her, and smiled. "I don't see why not." He was brown, and I thought he had lost some weight.

The saloon was a large dining room with some leather tub chairs, a green carpet, a radiogram, and one or two tapestries on the walls. What really astonished me about it was that it had a fireplace.

Roger was leaning against the table talking to an Alison elegant and business-like in splendidly cut slacks and an oyster jersey. When she saw Hugh she beckoned to him. Willingly he went to her.

"You don't want to be tied to your mother's apron strings, do you?" she said.

"No."

"You're too much of a man for that. So you come in with me. Besides, your things won't be such a nuisance. "The idea," Alison said, "of sharing a cabin with another woman — and imagination *fails* me! The other two will just have to make do."

For the second time recently, though from so different a cause, my heart lurched, and began to beat faster. The merest change of expression had crossed Joanna's face, but she didn't look at me.

"What are lee boards for?" Hugh was asking Roger.

"You lower them into the water to reduce drift. You get drift with a keel-less craft."

"What is keel-less?"

* * * * *

I had undressed and lay on the lower bunk. Joanna had asked for the top one. It was only with lying down I had come to realize I was tired from a first day living at sea. The yacht moved slightly, and water lapped against its side.

I can no longer recall all the details of how even that first day was filled; which became progressively more true of the holiday as a whole. (It never entered my head, I suppose it was stupid, at any rate unprescient, that I could conceivably some time want it as background material.)

Perhaps this says something about me; perhaps it says something about the nature of long-term memory, which has always seemed to me like walking on a bright day through a deep forest with intermittent, apparently arbitrary, stretches and patches of sunlight. For instance, I know that we docked at a place called Lorient, but I remember nothing about it at all — not even, without looking, whether it came before or after Dinard, a very French sophisticated town, and, when I saw it, with sun glittering on the sea.

That I remember in it's entirety what happened with Joanna surely says something about the nature of being in love.

Though tired, I was intensely aware of her presence in the cabin, her movements, her breathing — almost the way one can listen, alert and motionless, to catch some distant sound.

She had been writing a postcard, seated in one of the cabin's small wicker chairs. More thinking than writing. Suddenly she handed the card to me. It was of a sad, tethered zebra, its head and flanks forlornly drooping. I looked at it, then turned the card over. I wasn't sure whether I was intended to read what had been written. It was addressed to her mother.

I read the printed explanatory paragraph. It said: "This miniature by Mansur, a renowned Mugal artist, was painted in 1612 for the Emperor Jahangir and was kept at the Imperial Courts at Agra and Delhi." I looked at the zebra again, then returned to the paragraph. "Jahangir's reign saw the height of Mugal art."

Oddly, I remember those words.

"It's nice."

"I'll finish it tomorrow. The zebra's sad."

I glanced up. She was standing with nothing on, holding her pajamas, her expression uncertain.

I gazed at her, the feelings created in me at this seemed to melt, to dissolve, to run warm through my whole being.

"I don't want to be coy," she said. "I just want you to love me."

I tried to say, "Come here," but something happened to the "come." I held out my hand. She came to me. I made space for her.

"What a lot of time we've wasted," she murmured it against my mouth. "Oh, Roz. Roz."

I don't know how long it was we just lay close. I know I said, "Are you cold?"

"A bit. It is your destiny to save me from the cold."

I put the blanket higher up round her. "If you *will* stand about with no clothes on."

She said then, a trace of laughter in her voice, but the voice unsure, as though it could as easily have been tears, "It's like your bloody car. There's not enough room. Do you know why I said 'bloody'?"

"No. I didn't think it was one of your words."

"Bill told me it's what yachtsmen call the sea — the bloody 'oggin."

"Hugh will love that."

At this there was a silence. She said, "I'm sorry about Hugh. Roz, I didn't mean it to happen."

"I know. Why didn't you say it before?"

"That I am sorry?"

"Anything."

"I don't know. I think I was angry that you were angry. No, that's not it. I don't know."

"I don't know either. About me. It doesn't matter now." I took her face between my hands and systematically kissed it, returning to the little scar. "Have you told your mother about *The Gold Digger*?"

"No. I'm going to send her a card from every port so that she will be truly amazed. I wish you knew my mother." She thought about this. Then she said, "Roz, do you think Alison meant what she was doing? I mean, letting us come in here. Was it for us, I mean?"

I smiled. "Or was it for Alison? Who knows?"

"I would have been terrified to go in with Alison. I would have been terrified to turn over for fear I wasn't doing it right."

"Hugh didn't mind. He was quite thrilled. Alison was terrific with Hugh."

I was touching the nape of her neck, caressing, incredulous of the joy, letting my hand follow the line of her spine, her skin cool, down, over that to me most erotic and beautiful part of her body, down to the small hollows behind her knees and back, stroking her.

I tried to think of the word I wanted, not slang, not colloquial even, the right word, but I couldn't find one. "Buttocks" was an infinity away from the joyous, grateful sexual response I felt.

"What are you thinking about?"

"Words."

"Oh, *Roz.*"

"About you, really. That there are no words for how beautiful and marvelous you are." I stroked her. She gave a small shiver.

"Shall I put a 'CLOSED' notice on the door?"

"Lock it. We'll only open up for Hugh."

"Do you care who knows about us?"

"No. Not now."

"Because of Mrs. Hallam? And Cassie? Because it isn't their business any more?"

"Partly that, but because, Joey, I love you."

It was a crucial moment. We both knew it.

We made love to each other then.

Afterwards, still in each other's arms, we talked as if we had a lifetime to make up for. As we talked she said suddenly, "Let's just stay here for the rest of the holiday. Do you think anyone would notice?"

"Not for a minute."

"Oh, but I can't," she said. "I've promised to help Bill with the water. It's a great system, Roz. It keeps the drinking water separate. Oh, and — but will you promise, will you absolutely promise not to say 'What nonsense!'? I am to be responsible for the safety drill."

"I won't say it."

"And I will be dedicated. I will be so dedicated, if only as a penance."

"Will you?" And I kissed her again. "Do you know, I once thought I would like to write a story of an American who went to Rome or Paris or somewhere —"

"Or Arcachon?"

"Yes, or Arcachon. And this American was agog for the trip but fell in love there and in the end didn't see anything but the inside of an attic."

"She did well. Was it a she?"

"Yes."

"Tell me when you want to go to sleep. I don't want to go to sleep. Not for ever."

"I don't want to go to sleep."

"Roz," she said, "do you know what the true test of a good lover is?"

"I couldn't guess."

She made a brief, mock show of clinging to me.

"It's not to fall over the edge."

SEVENTEEN

We grew accustomed to the roll of the yacht, which at times I thought fearsome, though Bill was of the opinion that we were lucky both ways considering it was "the turbulent Bay."

Hugh was the last to latch on firmly to the realization that putting things down on ledges and tables in no way ensured that they would stay there.

Roger and Peter became sailors overnight, or more accurately in the case of Peter, reverted to one.

With Joanna it was rather different. She simply adapted at once, with a practical enthusiasm quite beyond anything I had expected, to her new — this next — environment.

Alison, contrary to her intention, bought materials and began to paint.

I read a lot.

Cassie was the only one of us to be seriously bothered by sea-sickness. Joanna took her drinks of milk and barley water mixed, a remedy apparently one of the Mary and Joseph nuns had sworn by, and Cassie said this helped. But Bill said the only cure for sea-sickness was time, of varying lengths. It took Cassie until we had almost reached La Rochelle, then suddenly she was quite better, and eager to take us on a tour of the town, having read up about it.

Whenever the opportunity was there we would always go ashore, though as the holiday went on I noticed that we tended to spend less time ashore and more on board. This was particularly true of Alison — until we reached Carpe-Écluse.

I have never returned to any of these places but I would like to see La Rochelle again for its interesting port and its strange, arcaded streets. It has a Musée des Beaux Arts, the site of a medieval castle, and a very unornate cathedral. Cassie told us about the Protestant history of the town.

We were standing looking at some frieze or other in the cathedral when I saw Roger put his arm 'round Joanna and lowering his face rub his cheek momentarily against hers. It was no more than a passing affectionate gesture, I suppose not uncharming in its way. At any rate one or two people nearby looked benign. Joanna seemed scarcely to have noticed it, though she did smile in response to the smile of an elderly German woman.

After we had left the cathedral, Joanna and I went off on our own with a food shopping list given to me by Henry, who was looking after Hugh for the morning. I knew Roger was going straight back to the yacht for a refueling operation with Bill.

"Roger," she said as we walked, "thinks Barbary is a horse in Shakespeare. One of the *Henrys*."

"Oh?" I glanced at her. It was hot. I could smell the hot leather of her handbag.

"Shall we have a drink before we get these things?"

"Yes," she said. "Only won't Hugh be waiting for you?"

"Roger's promised to let him watch the refueling."

We went into the Café de la Paix, Café de la Poste, something like that. It had a rather dark, nineteenth-century interior, which was a relief after the sun.

"What do you want?"

"Orangina."

"*Orangina?* All right. Orangina.

The way the French waiter served us, it might have been champagne, as Joanna commented. We sat with our drinks.

"Joey, you know what we said about locking the cabin door?"

"Yes." She looked up. "Nobody seems to have taken the slightest interest in our cabin door."

"It's because they haven't noticed. But suppose they had. Could you take that?" I held her gaze. "It wouldn't be easy. It wouldn't be the rest of the world beaming its approval. As if it were you and Roger, say."

"Roger?" She smiled, then. "Or Henry? Or Bill? Roz, listen. I can't imagine my life without you. You are the only person in the world who really matters to me. Except, of course, my mother, and she will only look puzzled. My mother has a marvelous line in looking puzzled at the ways of others. But she would never interfere."

"I know I would like her."

"If you didn't mean so much to me, if you weren't everything to me, Roz, I think we wouldn't have survived Barbary. I think that was a kind of test." There was a pause.

"Something else." The thought came suddenly into my mind without, I think, my connivance. "Do you remember what you told me about Steve and being pregnant?"

"Yes." She was surprised.

I had to look for the words that followed. "Will you want to be? Pregnant."

The café all at once seemed to be very quiet. She moved something on the table. Then she said, "No one ever has everything." Quickly, as if that was that, she went on, her tone of voice changing a little, "Did you see those men on the quay painting their boat? You're not going to believe this. You'll think I'm inventing it because it fits, but I'm not. One of them was saying to the other one, 'She's a nice girl, she's a wonderful girl, there's just one thing, she doesn't seem to *understand* when you talk to her.' So — do you understand? In words of seven letters — no, sorry, eight — I love you."

"And I love you."

"On the way back I'm going to get a tin of paint. There's just one or two bits here and there need touching up on ours. Have you seen?"

Our waiter approached us. "Autre chose, mesdames?"

Joanna was adding, "It's a great feeling when those sails go up and the wind takes hold of them. I can't really explain it. I don't know why. It just makes me feel great."

What Hugh wanted to know on our return to the yacht was why I hadn't got back in time to see the refueling, which he said was "good."

Arcachon was a disappointment. Despite the magic its name had. There were some nice villas behind the sand dunes, and Cassie talked to us about the architecture in general, Louis XIV, Edwardian, but overpoweringly the place was a resort. Very commercial, very crowded. At the center of the town there was a casino, with a Moorish look about it, and the night we tied up in the harbor there Alison decided that she wanted to visit the casino.

But Hugh was very tired, and so I stayed on board with him. After I had read him a story he fell straight to sleep, and I went on deck to where Bill sat smoking a French cigarette, the smoke spreading out in the motionless air.

I said, really to make conversation, "Do you know what you're going to do after this?"

He looked at me, good-natured, keen-eyed. "Yes. It's all cut and dried. I'm taking her to New York," he said, speaking of the yacht. "And then we're booked up with Americans for a Canadian trip. Three doubles, and a single."

"It sounds marvelous."

He paused and nodded. "There's just one more thing I've got to get done before we go. A bit of carpentry, really. A couple of cabin extensions. That's all fixed." He put out his cigarette end and half smiled. "I would have been off sooner if it hadn't been for my arrangement with Mrs. Elliott."

"Your arrangement with Mrs. Elliott is working out very well. When *do* you expect to go?" I refused his offer of a cigarette, though I liked the smell.

"The Canada trip is to be September. Before the weather changes. And after that I'm already organized for the Caribbean." He talked, as always when it was to do with his yacht, easily and with a kind of implied pride.

"Where will you go in Canada?"

"Not entirely sure. Strait of Canso for the locks. The Saguenay Fjord. That's always a winner. The idea is not to be too tied down. We'll have the whole month to play with."

It was then that he added, "We might even branch out for a bit. A change of scene. Not that I've quite made up my mind about that yet."

* * * * *

Alison won a small fortune at the casino. The next day, a few miles further down the coast, we discovered by chance Carpe-Écluse. And, as she said, it might not have been Bormes-les-Mimosas but, by heavens, it would serve.

* * * * *

I have never been very visual in the sense of analyzing and being readily moved by "sights," but the sight of Carpe-Écluse moved me.

Alison did the analyzing, her eye delighted and absorbed as she spoke of "happy dimensions." The church, for instance, was not only perfect Norman — its arches rounded, its pillars sturdy — it was practically in the pocket of the busy, down-to-earth village hotel. The harbor was pretty with its colored sails and the changing colors of the water but it was a working harbor strewn with working equipment, and the brick cottages that backed it were almost severely functional. The silver-sanded beach was saved from being "postcard" by touches here and there of the rugged, the wild even, fierce rocks, coarse grass.

The port's showpiece, a trifle perversely in a port, was the river that ran throughout the town.

I think of Carpe-Écluse as an idyll. Not only because of the enchantment of the place itself but because of the change that, over a glass of Orangina, had occurred in me. I suppose it could only be said that I had taken the long way home when it came to arriving at the belief that Joanna and I were safe in our relationship, that there would be no outside threat. But in the end I *had* arrived at it, with all that this meant to my state of mind.

Some of the time during the day at Carpe-Écluse we spent apart. Often she would be with Bill and Henry, about the business of the yacht. I had no sense of unease. The nights were ours.

By unanimous agreement we dismissed all idea of going on to Biarritz, and stayed till the last possible moment in this magic corner of the French coast we had come upon so by chance.

The last afternoon we were there Joanna and I sat in the sun on deck where I had talked with Bill about his plans. Hugh, within the strict limits of what was safe on the yacht, played nearby.

"Roz —"

"Yes, darling?"

"If you hadn't married Tom would *you* have gone to university?"

"I suppose so. It was pretty standard for our final year."

"Did you have any idea what it was you wanted to do?"

"Not really. I knew I wanted to write something but that could hardly have counted."

"I still have absolutely no idea what it is I want to do."

"Now you've had time to think about it, or not think, but get the feel. How did the A Levels really go?"

"I felt," she said, "two of them were all right." She smiled. "After I'd finished the geography I was sure as a geographer I'd do well to map my way out of the hall."

I returned the smile. "I expect it only seemed like that. Geography was last, wasn't it? And you'd have been quite tired."

"What will I choose with English and sociology?"

"There are endless possibilities and you'll have a whole three years before you have to make up your mind about what you want to do." I found as I said this that my attitude to Joanna at university, no, not my attitude, but my feeling about it, had now also changed. Somehow it added to my feeling of safety. There she would be, somewhere quite close, for another three years, and often she would come to me, and it would be heaven, and such problems as we might eventually have, whatever these turned out to be, could at any rate be deferred. Solved.

She said, "Three years! Oh, Roz, it sounds forever."

Before I could reply to this Hugh came up to us. "I want," he said, "to see Mrs. Carnaby again. I want to send her a postcard."

"All right," Joanna said, turning to him. "Shall I help you write it? I mean, just write the address." Then she added, though in the voice of someone who doubted it was really going to get done, "I ought to write to Pauline."

Later that evening, in rather subdued mood, we had what amounted to a farewell party in the saloon, for which its bar had been very adequately "liquored up," to use Peter's expression. We could have gone ashore for the evening but somehow none of us wanted to; I think we had been caught, Alison too, not just by the simple life aboard, but by the autonomy of it. We were our own little world.

First we had special omelettes, which Henry allowed us as a concession, though he didn't approve of omelettes; then there was fruit, and from somewhere there came a huge jar of Canadian cracked nuts.

I remember that, amusing myself, I took twelve of the nuts and arranged them in a pattern of threes — Brazils, walnuts, hazels, almonds — and began to eat them in order. Joanna, sitting quietly with whatever she was drinking, watched me.

"Never in all my life," Alison was saying, "have I encountered such a collection of blasphemies and obscenities as are exchanged by seafarers. And the extraordinary thing is they all seem to understand one another, regardless of color, race or creed. I have heard foreign sailors addressed successively in good German, excellent French, and bawling standard English all to no purpose, only to find that when the water was referred to as 'bloody hoggin' they instantly grasped the situation, whatever it was."

" 'Oggin," Peter said.

"I said hoggin," Alison said. "Did I not say hoggin?" She turned to Roger. "I am in need of your moral support."

"Never," Roger said, "and, anyway, isn't that what you should give me? I'm sure it's the sort of thing you should only get from a mother." He kissed her cheek, and picked up her glass, asking the rest of us what we would have.

"Well —" Alison's eyes followed her glass. "I am beginning to experience a strange inner glow."

"I expect it's the nuts."

Alison glanced in Joanna's direction with something, I thought, of the look a batsman gives an unexpected ball, but good-humored, not unfriendly, though a little detached. It was the line she seemed to have taken with both of us since the holiday started, a subtle variation of her re-established habitual behavior towards me.

"Oh yes, of course," she said, "the nuts; how silly of me — I should have known."

And Roger said, "I wondered when it was that Joanna was going to say something."

"Well, now she has. It's a rare quality, only to say something when there's something to be said. And one I have never myself managed to cultivate."

"Oh I don't think I'd put it quite like that."

"But then we would expect you, Roz, to have alternative modes of expression at your command." Alison passed my glass to Roger.

Joanna said, "I think it's great, having an inner glow."

There was a pause which was ended simultaneously by Henry and Hugh.

Henry said, "We are out of washing-up liquid."

And Hugh, standing and looking up at one of the tapestries, said, "Why has that horse got a horn?"

"That horse has got a horn," Roger said, and suddenly he swung Hugh up to where he could get a better view of the tapestry, "because it is a unicorn. When I wash up I never bother with it." He glanced at Henry.

"What an excellent memory you have, Roger," Alison said. "Mind what you're doing with Hugh. We have never been given the slightest reason to suppose he's expendable."

"Still, it is a winning sight," Cassie said, half serious, "a young man good with children."

"I'm relying on it," Roger said.

However, Joanna was not attending to him. She was saying to Henry, "They were great omelettes, Henry. What was in them? Besides the artichokes?"

"Butter and cream and eggs," he said, without enthusiasm. "Seasoning."

"Yes, but they tasted of something else. What was it?"

"Chives," he said. "I expect you're talking about chives. It's not correct with Frittata al Carciofi. But I like to throw a few in."

"Well, they were great," she said again. She looked at him suddenly with her smile that was almost a laugh, the small expulsion of breath, and added, "Though are you sure we're getting enough chemicals with our food? Frittata al Carciofi. That reminds me," she went on almost to herself, and I realized that for the first time I was seeing her a little drunk, "I will give all my loose French change to anyone who can tell me what *The Plover* and Garbo have in common."

It was Bill who knew. "Both made in Sweden?"

"Always said he knows everything there is worth knowing," Roger commented.

"But I won't take your money."

She said, "I'll do the washing up instead. And to hell with the washing-up liquid."

Soon after this, Peter took a record from the small pile and put it on the radiogram. "Nothing like Cole Porter."

Roger refilled Joanna's glass. There was no room to dance in the saloon but clearly the music was creating in him the wish to do so. He tapped with his foot. "Let's go on deck," he said to her at length.

She went with him. If Alison raised an eyebrow very, very slightly in my direction, this was barely perceptible.

It was Hugh who said, "I want to go on deck, too."

Stars and velvet skies are, I suppose, the cliché of all time. But that's what it was like on deck. Hugh looked round him as we walked, then he said, "Can you buy unicorns?"

The music from the saloon was clearly audible. Now it was "I Get a Kick Out of You." I expected to find Roger and Joanna dancing. I didn't mind.

Then I became aware in the near darkness that we had approached them and that Roger, more decisive in his relations with her than I had known him before, had caught hold of her and was kissing her.

She didn't resist. She just appeared to wait until he had finished. Afterwards, conscious of my presence and Hugh's, she just said, "Roz —"

She hesitated for the merest instant, disengaged herself from Roger, walked over to me, put her arms round my neck and very deliberately, for a long time, kissed my mouth.

My response, unthought out and instinctive, was to welcome her into my arms.

Roger looked at us. For a moment or two there was silence, then he said, "O.K. O.K. Fair enough."

Hugh, occupied still with his own concern, was saying, "Well, can you? Buy them?"

Roger hadn't moved away.

*****

Two things I remember very particularly about the return to Southampton, one a detail, the other not, but that seems to be the way memory works. At Cherbourg we had the most marvelous stuffed aubergines I have ever tasted in my life; and before Cherbourg Hugh said he wanted to come and sleep in my cabin.

EIGHTEEN

My mother and father in their attitudes generally were not to be compared with Roger. Or for that matter with Alison. But they knew something of Joanna's story, and — I suppose it was another sign of being in love — when I wasn't with her I wanted to talk about her, and so I talked about her to them, in an edited sort of way.

They were always quite willing to talk. They had insisted that Hugh and I should go to them for a little while straight from Southampton, where I had left the car before *The Gold Digger* holiday, Swanage was comparatively only a few miles further on.

One or two mornings after Hugh and I had arrived we all went for a walk along the front. He didn't run on ahead as far as usual, but he did detach himself from us and quite happily went looking for shells. My parents had had a settling effect on him.

My mother said, "Well, I feel sorry for the girl. Her mother couldn't have thought much of her."

The morning seemed to be very every day English after our time abroad. A pale sheen of light clung to the hills like new plush, the sea and sky were joined in what appeared almost a single stretch of mild blue, and the rocks, the bay, the dips in the hills all stood out clearly, but in an unemphasized, almost throwaway fashion.

"I think it has been more a question of a terribly close relationship, so that she couldn't fit in with her mother's new life and the new man. Or she felt she couldn't. She did fly out to them once, but she said it didn't work." I added, "She thought the island was beautiful, and she liked the mopeds."

"Then she'll be making her home with her father now?"

"Oh, I think she'll stay with Cassie until she goes to university. Her father's away such a lot. And Cassie's liked having her."

"The young lady has decided on university after all, then?" my father said.

"She hasn't really; but I'm sure she will when she gets her results. Her father wants her to teach. I suppose he'd settle for commerce. But I can't imagine either." It was true that I wasn't sure what I could imagine for her. The B.B.C? Publishing, perhaps. For the first time since we had moved to Whitethorn it had entered my head as a possibility that maybe one day Hugh and I might move back to London.

"She'll be all right with a degree behind her. Take her pick," my father said. "And she should certainly be set up for any amount of hard work —"

"She *has* worked very hard."

"— after the trip you've just had. I've been calculating the number of miles you must have covered."

"It took for ever so long," Hugh said, coming up with a handful of shells.

My father looked at one of the shells. "*Phalium Labiatum.* Sandy bottoms," he said. "You were lucky not to have had any teething troubles over that distance. After all, it was by way of being a maiden voyage, wasn't it?"

"I think Bill Moon's had a very clear idea what he's about. He knows now he wants to squeeze some more storage space out of the yacht, and he's going to manage a couple more small cabins, I believe Joanna said. That's being done while he stays for a few days with Alison and James."

My father said, "It's odd what's come out of Roger taking that chap home."

"I wouldn't have guessed."

"Seeing into the future seems to run in families. But not in ours. Though Claudia," my mother added, speaking of her sister, "does sometimes seem to have a feeling about things. She knew before we did that Daddy and I were going to get married."

"And she didn't warn me," my father said, putting his arm around her. Hugh laughed.

When we got back to the house the phone was going. It was Joanna.

"Roz," she said. "Darling. There's something I must talk to you about. Something I want to tell you."

I was aware at once of a new quality in her voice, not excitement exactly — I had heard that before — more like drive. Puzzled, and wanting her to go on, I said, "Well — I'm here."

"No, I can't on the phone. I must see you. Everything's changed. It's terrific. Not that everyone thinks so. My father, for one. To put it like that. Still, I really can do what I like now. And Cassie's not very pleased. In fact, I'm at bay."

"You're what?"

"At bay. Come and be with me, Roz. Come and stand with me."

"Joey, what *are* you talking about?"

"Me. You. Come, and I'll tell you. Soon. The soonest. It has to be that. When can you come?"

"I could come any time. Hugh wants to stay on over the weekend with his grandparents. But —"

"Now? Tomorrow? Where could we meet?"

"Meet?"

"*I* want to see you first. I want to see you before anyone else does. I want it to be just us, Roz. Just us talking." She barely paused. "The Johnny Onion. When? What time?"

*****

She looked wonderful. Glowing and joyous. She was wearing a fir-green dress, open at the neck, and with a belt she had pulled rather tight; the dark color somehow accentuating her unused look. Briefly she buried her face into my neck. I don't know what the Frenchman thought, if anything. I know I didn't care.

"This time, Roz," she said, "we *must* have champagne." Then, over the ritual serving of the wine, the placing before us of salted almonds in a small pottery dish decorated with French flags, immediately she began to talk.

"I was looking at a map, I wanted to see how long the St. Lawrence actually was, because of Bill, and it suddenly dawned on me, it suddenly came to me, Roz, that if you drew a line across the sea from Halifax, say, to Hamilton, it wouldn't be very far at all, and if you did the trip the other way 'round, from New York, it would be even shorter. And I said to Bill, I all at once thought of it, just like that," — the words were as though they were running downhill — "I said, if you'll take in Bermuda I'll come with you. I'd be invaluable." She laughed. "Well, I'd be a better barmaid than Roger."

"Joanna —"

"At first he thought I wasn't serious — Bill, I mean. But when he found that I was, he was really quite quick to see the advantages, and, Roz, in the end he said all right, he said if Mrs. Elliott didn't mind, all right. And I'm nothing to do with Mrs. Elliott. So —"

I stared at her, disbelieving, trying to take in the significance of what so utterly out of the blue as far as I was concerned, she was saying.

"Oh, darling, don't look like that. It's for us. It's for both of us. I explained to Bill what an advantage it would be to have us. We could be terribly useful, we could do the shopping — Henry's hopeless at that — and generally fetch and carry and such, and I could do the women's hair; I often did Pauline's. And, oh, Roz, it would be *marvelous*, don't you see? Sailing the high seas and having a Great Adventure." She mocked her words with capital letters, but she meant them.

I continued to stare at her.

"Of course we'd have to make do," she said. "We couldn't take over cabins that Bill could sell. I mean we'd have to sleep in the saloon, maybe. But that's the thing about it. We could have this wonderful time and it wouldn't cost Bill anything. It would be all advantage to him. I'm sure rich people quite soon get tired of a hundred per cent self-service, whatever they may have thought. And we'd have each other. All night, Roz."

I said at last, "How could I do that? How could I just go away like that?"

"Easily, Roz. You could leave Peter to let your flat. It's all got to be quick, though. By Monday. Bill's sailing on Monday. But you could do it easily. You can write anywhere. We don't have to make preparations. Just a toothbrush and a few clothes. We can buy anything we need in New York. I've arranged for money there."

Money, it passed stupidly in and out of my mind. What's money go to do with it? I was about to say, "How can I take Hugh?" when, not thinking what I was doing, I caught my glass with my elbow, tipping it over. The wine spread across the tablecloth. In an instant the Frenchman had removed the cloth, murmuring apologies, and had replaced it with a clean one.

"Voila!"

It was as if she knew what I had been about to say, "And Hugh could go in with Henry. Henry and Roger managed all right. Hugh quite liked Henry. We could promote him to second mate."

"But, Joanna —" feeling what I had to say was so obvious, I still didn't know what to say first — "— it's nothing to do with Henry. I can't simply take Hugh off 'round the world like that. How could I? He's just settled down in school, apart from anything else. And that was hard enough for him. And —"

"He'd learn much more going 'round the world than he'll ever learn at school in Whitethorn. And we could teach him. So many hours a day." She smiled, persuasively. "He could end up a wonderful sociologist. And the geography would take care of itself."

"I couldn't do that, Joey. You can't just do things like that with a little boy. Really, you can't."

She hesitated. "Aren't you going to make patterns with your almonds?" she said, before she added, "It would mean I could see my mother. Not some hard and fast arrangement of weeks where you have to go through with it whatever it's like, not like the last time, but I could just call in because I happened to be there. Not gift wrapped. And we could see how it went. There wouldn't have to be a *situation,* you understand what I mean, Roz? We could just have a coffee. I could always say there were things I had to do on the yacht. Oh, it would be wonderful, Roz, seeing her like that. You must understand that."

I did understand it.

As I looked at her my sensation of having been taken totally by surprise, almost ambushed, I think, became something else, perhaps the first faint perception of what it was *she* was feeling.

Even as I said it I knew how absurd it was, how useless it was, to point out that she hadn't even had her A Level results.

"Oh, those," she said. "Well, that's in the past. I can't alter that. It's tomorrow that matters. Come with me. Come and be 'us' together in the next part of our lives. Please, Roz."

There was a long, long silence. The champagne at my side, untouched, seemed to grow flatter.

She said, "I can't spend the rest of my life in Whitethorn. You must see that. And I know really I can't spend three years of it in some lecture hall. Don't start saying no to things again, Roz. You didn't do it to me. Don't do it now. Nothing's safe. Only yesterday's safe."

The silence on my side just went on and on.

Finally she said, "I want to see my mother. Come on, Roz, let's go home. I don't want this." As she pushed her glass aside, I saw what I had done to her joy.

At home, the house was empty. Cassie had gone to London to meet Peter, and they were having dinner with friends.

The evening passed somehow. We made eggs, cheese, on toast, I don't remember, but neither of us wanted it. Though we talked, it served only to reveal further how irreconcilable our positions were. I couldn't give way, because the decision wasn't for me. And I believe that on her side, for whatever reasons, needs, I don't know, she truly couldn't, either.

As it grew dark we knew without speaking of it that we were not going to spend the night separately.

Returning from the bathroom I found her seated on the bed. She sat with her legs under her, leaning back a little, supporting herself on her hands, her face momentarily averted, pressed against a shoulder so that her hair, not cut since we came back from France, fell over arm and shoulder. Her skin was a holiday mix of pale and brown.

Though I wasn't aware of it, I think subconsciously I sought then to memorize her; the small breasts, the slight inclines to her waist, the tender triangle of hair.

She said, "If I hadn't known I wouldn't have thought of you as having a dressing gown that color. Can I take it with me?"

"Don't go."

"I have to go. It's where life's taking me." Then, much I think, as I had raised the issue of her A Levels, without expectation, she added, "Could Hugh stay with your parents? He loves your parents."

"Joey, he's my son."

She looked down in an attempt to conceal the tears that had suddenly filled her eyes. For only the second time in my experience of her there were tears. The first time seemed far away. I sat down by her.

I lifted her face. "Listen. Darling, listen. It was terrible for Hugh when Tom was killed. Terrifying. He —"

But she didn't let me finish. "I know, I know." Then facing me, the direct look which was so familiar, she said, "It's not forever. It's not for long. I'll come back, Roz. I will. I'll come back to *you*." She pushed my dressing gown off, back over my shoulders.

I had always loved it when she undressed me, the exchanging of clothes for her hands and mouth, the delight of referred pleasure, the delight of giving as well as taking.

She made love to me with the skill she had learned over months, and with a demanding intensity which had nothing to do with anything learned, as if to say, "This I will have," covering my body with hers, leaving no part of me, it seemed, unclaimed, unpossessed.

Distantly, I half heard Peter put his car away in the garage as I held her.

Afterwards other things happened. Her father phoned again, telling her, I gathered, in short, uncompromising sentences what a mess she was about to make of her life. Monday came. Later in the month I went to Mrs. Hallam's cottage to find out about her results. The *1905* under the eaves had faded further in the summer sun.

Telling me about the two As and the B, Mrs. Hallam said, "She did well. We can be proud of her. She could have taken her pick with those grades. Oxford or Cambridge. But —" she smiled a little wryly, "— at least she'll be in a position to change her mind. For now we must just leave her to get on with her life in her own way. Mustn't we?"

She went on to tell me she had seen Alison in the Columbine that morning. "The lift —" she began. But something in my expression perhaps stopped her because then, taking hold of both my hands, she drew me into her haphazardly furnished sitting room.

"Sit down, Roz," she said. "I'll make some tea and we can talk."

Only what was there to say, except that Joanna was being Joanna, and I loved her?

* * * * *

It appeared that she went on being Joanna. She wrote to me, quite short letters, but often at first. Seeing her mother was great. She had learned to drive a Bermudian horse carriage.

Then she was working with a fringe theatre — a children's club — something to do with American T.V. America was great, too.

The Gold Digger again. Nevis. St. Kitts.

Gradually the letters became fewer. And then they stopped. Once she had said something about coming back, but she didn't come. I didn't see her again.

EPILOGUE

Had the story been written when Joanna had gone, or for a long time after that, it would for me have been a sad, even a despairing one. Tritely, I recall, I played Sinatra's "That Rainy Day" to echo the desolation of not having her.

But now, so many years on, I see that it is not a sad story, and that I was not playing the right record. It should have been, "I Didn't Know What Time It Was."

I hadn't known what time it was, then I met her. The story is to celebrate that. To celebrate, I suppose, Joanna herself, who had been the lovely means whereby I had found my way into the warm world of sexual loving and without whom I am sure my life would have been so different, colder.

Though I didn't know when I started it, I know now that I have written the story to say thank you.

A few of the publications of

THE NAIAD PRESS, INC.

P.O. Box 10543 • Tallahassee, Florida 32302

Phone (904) 539-5965

Mail orders welcome. Please include 15% postage.

IN THE BLOOD by Lauren Wright Douglas. 252 pp. Lesbian science fiction adventure fantasy	ISBN 0-941483-22-3	$8.95
THE BEE'S KISS by Shirley Verel. 216 pp. Delicate, delicious romance.	ISBN 0-941483-36-3	8.95
RAGING MOTHER MOUNTAIN by Pat Emmerson. 264 pp. Furosa Firechild's adventures in Wonderland.	ISBN 0-941483-35-5	8.95
IN EVERY PORT by Karin Kallmaker. 228 pp. Jessica's sexy, adventuresome travels.	ISBN 0-941483-37-7	8.95
OF LOVE AND GLORY by Evelyn Kennedy. 192 pp. Exciting WWII romance.	ISBN 0-941483-32-0	8.95
CLICKING STONES by Nancy Tyler Glenn. 288 pp. Love transcending time.	ISBN 0-941483-31-2	8.95
SURVIVING SISTERS by Gail Pass. 252 pp. Powerful love story.	ISBN 0-941483-16-9	8.95
SOUTH OF THE LINE by Catherine Ennis. 216 pp. Civil War adventure.	ISBN 0-941483-29-0	8.95
WOMAN PLUS WOMAN by Dolores Klaich. 300 pp. Supurb Lesbian overview.	ISBN 0-941483-28-2	9.95
SLOW DANCING AT MISS POLLY'S by Sheila Ortiz Taylor. 96 pp. Lesbian Poetry	ISBN 0-941483-30-4	7.95
DOUBLE DAUGHTER by Vicki P. McConnell. 216 pp. A Nyla Wade Mystery, third in the series.	ISBN 0-941483-26-6	8.95
HEAVY GILT by Delores Klaich. 192 pp. Lesbian detective/ disappearing homophobes/upper class gay society.	ISBN 0-941483-25-8	8.95
THE FINER GRAIN by Denise Ohio. 216 pp. Brilliant young college lesbian novel.	ISBN 0-941483-11-8	8.95
THE AMAZON TRAIL by Lee Lynch. 216 pp. Life, travel & lore of famous lesbian author.	ISBN 0-941483-27-4	8.95
HIGH CONTRAST by Jessie Lattimore. 264 pp. Women of the Crystal Palace.	ISBN 0-941483-17-7	8.95
OCTOBER OBSESSION by Meredith More. Josie's rich, secret Lesbian life.	ISBN 0-941483-18-5	8.95
LESBIAN CROSSROADS by Ruth Baetz. 276 pp. Contemporary Lesbian lives.	ISBN 0-941483-21-5	9.95

BEFORE STONEWALL: THE MAKING OF A GAY AND LESBIAN COMMUNITY by Andrea Weiss & Greta Schiller. 96 pp., 25 illus. ISBN 0-941483-20-7 7.95

WE WALK THE BACK OF THE TIGER by Patricia A. Murphy. 192 pp. Romantic Lesbian novel/beginning women's movement. ISBN 0-941483-13-4 8.95

SUNDAY'S CHILD by Joyce Bright. 216 pp. Lesbian athletics, at last the novel about sports. ISBN 0-941483-12-6 8.95

OSTEN'S BAY by Zenobia N. Vole. 204 pp. Sizzling adventure romance set on Bonaire. ISBN 0-941483-15-0 8.95

LESSONS IN MURDER by Claire McNab. 216 pp. 1st in a stylish mystery series. ISBN 0-941483-14-2 8.95

YELLOWTHROAT by Penny Hayes. 240 pp. Margarita, bandit, kidnaps Julia. ISBN 0-941483-10-X 8.95

SAPPHISTRY: THE BOOK OF LESBIAN SEXUALITY by Pat Califia. 3d edition, revised. 208 pp. ISBN 0-941483-24-X 8.95

CHERISHED LOVE by Evelyn Kennedy. 192 pp. Erotic Lesbian love story. ISBN 0-941483-08-8 8.95

LAST SEPTEMBER by Helen R. Hull. 208 pp. Six stories & a glorious novella. ISBN 0-941483-09-6 8.95

THE SECRET IN THE BIRD by Camarin Grae. 312 pp. Striking, psychological suspense novel. ISBN 0-941483-05-3 8.95

TO THE LIGHTNING by Catherine Ennis. 208 pp. Romantic Lesbian 'Robinson Crusoe' adventure. ISBN 0-941483-06-1 8.95

THE OTHER SIDE OF VENUS by Shirley Verel. 224 pp. Luminous, romantic love story. ISBN 0-941483-07-X 8.95

DREAMS AND SWORDS by Katherine V. Forrest. 192 pp. Romantic, erotic, imaginative stories. ISBN 0-941483-03-7 8.95

MEMORY BOARD by Jane Rule. 336 pp. Memorable novel about an aging Lesbian couple. ISBN 0-941483-02-9 8.95

THE ALWAYS ANONYMOUS BEAST by Lauren Wright Douglas. 224 pp. A Caitlin Reese mystery. First in a series. ISBN 0-941483-04-5 8.95

SEARCHING FOR SPRING by Patricia A. Murphy. 224 pp. Novel about the recovery of love. ISBN 0-941483-00-2 8.95

DUSTY'S QUEEN OF HEARTS DINER by Lee Lynch. 240 pp. Romantic blue-collar novel. ISBN 0-941483-01-0 8.95

PARENTS MATTER by Ann Muller. 240 pp. Parents' relationships with Lesbian daughters and gay sons. ISBN 0-930044-91-6 9.95

THE PEARLS by Shelley Smith. 176 pp. Passion and fun in the Caribbean sun. ISBN 0-930044-93-2 7.95

MAGDALENA by Sarah Aldridge. 352 pp. Epic Lesbian novel set on three continents. ISBN 0-930044-99-1 8.95

THE BLACK AND WHITE OF IT by Ann Allen Shockley. 144 pp. Short stories. ISBN 0-930044-96-7 7.95

SAY JESUS AND COME TO ME by Ann Allen Shockley. 288 pp. Contemporary romance. ISBN 0-930044-98-3 8.95

LOVING HER by Ann Allen Shockley. 192 pp. Romantic love story. ISBN 0-930044-97-5 7.95

MURDER AT THE NIGHTWOOD BAR by Katherine V. Forrest. 240 pp. A Kate Delafield mystery. Second in a series. ISBN 0-930044-92-4 8.95

ZOE'S BOOK by Gail Pass. 224 pp. Passionate, obsessive love story. ISBN 0-930044-95-9 7.95

WINGED DANCER by Camarin Grae. 228 pp. Erotic Lesbian adventure story. ISBN 0-930044-88-6 8.95

PAZ by Camarin Grae. 336 pp. Romantic Lesbian adventurer with the power to change the world. ISBN 0-930044-89-4 8.95

SOUL SNATCHER by Camarin Grae. 224 pp. A puzzle, an adventure, a mystery — Lesbian romance. ISBN 0-930044-90-8 8.95

THE LOVE OF GOOD WOMEN by Isabel Miller. 224 pp. Long-awaited new novel by the author of the beloved *Patience and Sarah.* ISBN 0-930044-81-9 8.95

THE HOUSE AT PELHAM FALLS by Brenda Weathers. 240 pp. Suspenseful Lesbian ghost story. ISBN 0-930044-79-7 7.95

HOME IN YOUR HANDS by Lee Lynch. 240 pp. More stories from the author of *Old Dyke Tales.* ISBN 0-930044-80-0 7.95

EACH HAND A MAP by Anita Skeen. 112 pp. Real-life poems that touch us all. ISBN 0-930044-82-7 6.95

SURPLUS by Sylvia Stevenson. 342 pp. A classic early Lesbian novel. ISBN 0-930044-78-9 7.95

PEMBROKE PARK by Michelle Martin. 256 pp. Derring-do and daring romance in Regency England. ISBN 0-930044-77-0 7.95

THE LONG TRAIL by Penny Hayes. 248 pp. Vivid adventures of two women in love in the old west. ISBN 0-930044-76-2 8.95

HORIZON OF THE HEART by Shelley Smith. 192 pp. Hot romance in summertime New England. ISBN 0-930044-75-4 7.95

AN EMERGENCE OF GREEN by Katherine V. Forrest. 288 pp. Powerful novel of sexual discovery. ISBN 0-930044-69-X 8.95

THE LESBIAN PERIODICALS INDEX edited by Claire Potter. 432 pp. Author & subject index. ISBN 0-930044-74-6 29.95

DESERT OF THE HEART by Jane Rule. 224 pp. A classic; basis for the movie *Desert Hearts.* ISBN 0-930044-73-8 7.95

SPRING FORWARD/FALL BACK by Sheila Ortiz Taylor. 288 pp. Literary novel of timeless love. ISBN 0-930044-70-3 7.95

FOR KEEPS by Elisabeth Nonas. 144 pp. Contemporary novel about losing and finding love. ISBN 0-930044-71-1 7.95

TORCHLIGHT TO VALHALLA by Gale Wilhelm. 128 pp. Classic novel by a great Lesbian writer. ISBN 0-930044-68-1 7.95

LESBIAN NUNS: BREAKING SILENCE edited by Rosemary Curb and Nancy Manahan. 432 pp. Unprecedented autobiographies of religious life. ISBN 0-930044-62-2 9.95

THE SWASHBUCKLER by Lee Lynch. 288 pp. Colorful novel set in Greenwich Village in the sixties. ISBN 0-930044-66-5 8.95

MISFORTUNE'S FRIEND by Sarah Aldridge. 320 pp. Historical Lesbian novel set on two continents. ISBN 0-930044-67-3 7.95

A STUDIO OF ONE'S OWN by Ann Stokes. Edited by Dolores Klaich. 128 pp. Autobiography. ISBN 0-930044-64-9 7.95

SEX VARIANT WOMEN IN LITERATURE by Jeannette Howard Foster. 448 pp. Literary history. ISBN 0-930044-65-7 8.95

A HOT-EYED MODERATE by Jane Rule. 252 pp. Hard-hitting essays on gay life; writing; art. ISBN 0-930044-57-6 7.95

INLAND PASSAGE AND OTHER STORIES by Jane Rule. 288 pp. Wide-ranging new collection. ISBN 0-930044-56-8 7.95

WE TOO ARE DRIFTING by Gale Wilhelm. 128 pp. Timeless Lesbian novel, a masterpiece. ISBN 0-930044-61-4 6.95

AMATEUR CITY by Katherine V. Forrest. 224 pp. A Kate Delafield mystery. First in a series. ISBN 0-930044-55-X 7.95

THE SOPHIE HOROWITZ STORY by Sarah Schulman. 176 pp. Engaging novel of madcap intrigue. ISBN 0-930044-54-1 7.95

THE BURNTON WIDOWS by Vickie P. McConnell. 272 pp. A Nyla Wade mystery, second in the series. ISBN 0-930044-52-5 7.95

OLD DYKE TALES by Lee Lynch. 224 pp. Extraordinary stories of our diverse Lesbian lives. ISBN 0-930044-51-7 8.95

DAUGHTERS OF A CORAL DAWN by Katherine V. Forrest. 240 pp. Novel set in a Lesbian new world. ISBN 0-930044-50-9 7.95

THE PRICE OF SALT by Claire Morgan. 288 pp. A milestone novel, a beloved classic. ISBN 0-930044-49-5 8.95

AGAINST THE SEASON by Jane Rule. 224 pp. Luminous, complex novel of interrelationships. ISBN 0-930044-48-7 8.95

LOVERS IN THE PRESENT AFTERNOON by Kathleen Fleming. 288 pp. A novel about recovery and growth. ISBN 0-930044-46-0 8.95

TOOTHPICK HOUSE by Lee Lynch. 264 pp. Love between two Lesbians of different classes. ISBN 0-930044-45-2 7.95

MADAME AURORA by Sarah Aldridge. 256 pp. Historical novel featuring a charismatic "seer." ISBN 0-930044-44-4 7.95

CURIOUS WINE by Katherine V. Forrest. 176 pp. Passionate Lesbian love story, a best-seller. ISBN 0-930044-43-6 8.95

BLACK LESBIAN IN WHITE AMERICA by Anita Cornwell. 141 pp. Stories, essays, autobiography. ISBN 0-930044-41-X 7.50

CONTRACT WITH THE WORLD by Jane Rule. 340 pp. Powerful, panoramic novel of gay life. ISBN 0-930044-28-2 7.95

YANTRAS OF WOMANLOVE by Tee A. Corinne. 64 pp. Photos by noted Lesbian photographer. ISBN 0-930044-30-4 6.95

MRS. PORTER'S LETTER by Vicki P. McConnell. 224 pp. The first Nyla Wade mystery. ISBN 0-930044-29-0 7.95

TO THE CLEVELAND STATION by Carol Anne Douglas. 192 pp. Interracial Lesbian love story. ISBN 0-930044-27-4 6.95

THE NESTING PLACE by Sarah Aldridge. 224 pp. A three-woman triangle—love conquers all! ISBN 0-930044-26-6 7.95

THIS IS NOT FOR YOU by Jane Rule. 284 pp. A letter to a beloved is also an intricate novel. ISBN 0-930044-25-8 8.95

FAULTLINE by Sheila Ortiz Taylor. 140 pp. Warm, funny, literate story of a startling family. ISBN 0-930044-24-X 6.95

THE LESBIAN IN LITERATURE by Barbara Grier. 3d ed. Foreword by Maida Tilchen. 240 pp. Comprehensive bibliography. Literary ratings; rare photos. ISBN 0-930044-23-1 7.95

ANNA'S COUNTRY by Elizabeth Lang. 208 pp. A woman finds her Lesbian identity. ISBN 0-930044-19-3 6.95

PRISM by Valerie Taylor. 158 pp. A love affair between two women in their sixties. ISBN 0-930044-18-5 6.95

BLACK LESBIANS: AN ANNOTATED BIBLIOGRAPHY compiled by J. R. Roberts. Foreword by Barbara Smith. 112 pp. Award-winning bibliography. ISBN 0-930044-21-5 5.95

THE MARQUISE AND THE NOVICE by Victoria Ramstetter. 108 pp. A Lesbian Gothic novel. ISBN 0-930044-16-9 4.95

OUTLANDER by Jane Rule. 207 pp. Short stories and essays by one of our finest writers. ISBN 0-930044-17-7 8.95

ALL TRUE LOVERS by Sarah Aldridge. 292 pp. Romantic novel set in the 1930s and 1940s. ISBN 0-930044-10-X 7.95

A WOMAN APPEARED TO ME by Renee Vivien. 65 pp. A classic; translated by Jeannette H. Foster. ISBN 0-930044-06-1 5.00

CYTHEREA'S BREATH by Sarah Aldridge. 240 pp. Romantic novel about women's entrance into medicine. ISBN 0-930044-02-9 6.95

TOTTIE by Sarah Aldridge. 181 pp. Lesbian romance in the turmoil of the sixties.	ISBN 0-930044-01-0	6.95
THE LATECOMER by Sarah Aldridge. 107 pp. A delicate love story.	ISBN 0-930044-00-2	5.00
ODD GIRL OUT by Ann Bannon.	ISBN 0-930044-83-5	5.95
I AM A WOMAN by Ann Bannon.	ISBN 0-930044-84-3	5.95
WOMEN IN THE SHADOWS by Ann Bannon.	ISBN 0-930044-85-1	5.95
JOURNEY TO A WOMAN by Ann Bannon.	ISBN 0-930044-86-X	5.95
BEEBO BRINKER by Ann Bannon.	ISBN 0-930044-87-8	5.95

Legendary novels written in the fifties and sixties, set in the gay mecca of Greenwich Village.

VOLUTE BOOKS

JOURNEY TO FULFILLMENT	Early classics by Valerie	3.95
A WORLD WITHOUT MEN	Taylor: The Erika Frohmann	3.95
RETURN TO LESBOS	series.	3.95

These are just a few of the many Naiad Press titles — we are the oldest and largest lesbian/feminist publishing company in the world. Please request a complete catalog. We offer personal service; we encourage and welcome direct mail orders from individuals who have limited access to bookstores carrying our publications.